A DREAM COME TRUE

With her heart fluttering, Kiki opened the door and made her entrance. Kyle's blue-green eyes met hers, and his face broke into a dazzling smile. Gosh, Kiki thought dreamily, he's even more handsome in person than in the movies.

Suddenly, Kiki's mind went completely blank. My line, she thought frantically, what's my line?

"I—I *am* sorry," she muttered. "I forgot my line."

He reached out and took her hand. "You look a little nervous," he said. "Is everything okay?"

Being so close to Kyle made Kiki tingle all over. "It's just . . . your eyes," she blurted. "I didn't expect them to be so blue."

His smile seemed to sparkle like a string of rhinestones. "Miss Adair, I'm awfully glad fate has brought us together." He lifted her hand gently to his lips and brushed it with a tender kiss . . .

STAR STRUCK

#4

Written by Fran Lantz

Created by
Eileen Goudge

AN AVON FLARE BOOK

SWEPT AWAY #4: STAR STRUCK is an original publication of Avon
Books. This work has never before appeared in book form.

AVON BOOKS
A division of
The Hearst Corporation
1790 Broadway
New York, New York 10019

First Flare Printing: January 1987

FLARE TRADEMARK REG. U.S. PAT. OFF. AND IN OTHER COUNTRIES,
MARCA REGISTRADA, HECHO EN U.S.A.

PRINTED IN THE U.S.A.

K-R 10 9 8 7 6 5 4 3 2 1

Chapter One

KIKI WYKOWSKI LIFTED THE HEM OF HER sequined gown and slid into the back seat of the limousine. Her date greeted her with a kiss that made her tingle all over.

"Hello, beautiful," he murmured. "You look fabulous . . . as usual."

"Thanks, Tommy." Dressed in a tuxedo, the movie superstar was twice as handsome in person as up on the screen.

Kiki slipped off her sunglasses, relaxing against the soft leather seat. From the limo's one-way windows, she could look out yet remain hidden from the autograph hounds who chased her everywhere she went. What a night!

As the limousine cruised through the palm-lined streets of Beverly Hills, Kiki watched the searchlights flashing across the velvety black sky, heralding the premiere of her latest film. Butterflies crowded her stomach. Would the critics love this one as much as the last one?

Minutes later, the limo glided to a stop in front of Grauman's Chinese Theatre, and Kiki stepped out into an explosion of flashbulbs.

"There she is!" someone shouted. "It's *her!*"

The crowd behind the velvet ropes pressed closer, clamoring for her autograph. Kiki could feel Tom's strong hand on her elbow, guiding her down the red-carpeted runway. She felt a surge of happiness. She had it all! She was a star!

Then Kiki spotted a teenage girl holding out an autograph book. Her wistful expression reminded Kiki of herself before she'd become famous, when she'd lived over her parents' deli, dreaming amidst the pumpernickel and corned beef of the glitter and fortune that awaited her in Hollywood. Kiki paused long enough to take the pen and—

Crash! Kiki's kitten leapt off the windowsill, terrified, and disappeared under the bed. The limousine, the crowd, the Beverly Hills movie theater all melted back into Kiki's imagination as she stared around her tiny bedroom. She could hear her little sisters yelling at each other in the room next to hers. "You kicked my blocks!" five-year-old Mimi wailed.

"Did not," seven-year-old Jenna retorted. "I just tripped on your stupid old doll."

"Spot is not stupid!" Mimi sniffled.

"Is too. Besides, who ever heard of a doll named Spot? That's a dog's name."

With a sigh, Kiki got up from her bed and went into her sisters' room. "Jenna, stop teasing Mimi," she said firmly. "Mimi, don't worry about your blocks. You can always build something else."

2

"Come help," said Mimi. "I can't make them stand up right."

"Yeah," agreed Jenna. "Help her build one of those big castles like you did last week. Then maybe she'll stop bothering *me*."

Kiki frowned. "Not today, Mimi. I have to help out in the store pretty soon." She pushed her shoulder-length, dark brown hair behind her ears as she went back to her own room. The sounds of her parents working in the family store, Nick's Eastside Delicatessen, drifted up the stairs to her. She could hear the familiar buzz of the meat slicer, the jingle of the bell above the door signaling that another lunchtime customer had just walked in, and her mother's cheerful voice asking, "Do you want mayo or mustard on that corned-beef sandwich?"

Kiki groaned as she lowered the needle onto her favorite Barbra Streisand record. Lying back on her bed, she gazed at the photos of famous actresses, past and present, that covered her walls. Judy Garland and Katharine Hepburn smiled at her from above the stereo. Meryl Streep and Jessica Lange hung above the night table. If only I could get away from here, Kiki thought longingly.

It wasn't that Kiki didn't love her parents or their little house in East Westdale. But she had dreams—big dreams—and they weren't getting any more real by making coleslaw in Nick's Deli. No one ever got to be a movie star by hanging around Westdale, Connecticut. *Hollywood*, she thought to herself. *That's where the action is, where the stars live, where the movies get made. And that's where I should be right now!*

Kiki smiled as Streisand's full, rich voice came through the headphones, singing "Somewhere," from the musical *West Side Story*. Oz jumped onto the bed, lay down on Kiki's stomach, and began purring happily.

"Listen to this, Oz," she said with awe. "Isn't she incredible?" Oz twitched her ears and purred louder.

Kiki giggled. Ever since her boyfriend, Steve Goldman, had given her the kitten for Christmas, she'd been having one-sided conversations with her pet. It was silly, she knew, but there was something about the look in the cat's big green eyes that almost made her believe she understood. In any case, talking to her helped Kiki sort out her feelings about things that were bothering her. These days, that meant just about everything—her career as an actress, her relationship with her parents, even the way things were going with Steve.

Kiki thought about her boyfriend, picturing his good-natured smile, his clear green eyes and his shock of wavy blond hair. He was such a nice guy but . . . she sighed in exasperation. Just like everything in Westdale, he was so unexciting and unromantic compared to the way she imagined life in Hollywood.

Kiki pushed her unhappy thoughts out of her mind, folded her hands behind her head, and hummed along with the record. She'd played the leading role in *West Side Story* last year, when

O. Henry High had put on the play, so she knew all the music. "Somewhere" was her favorite song. It was so beautiful it almost hurt.

Kiki smiled, remembering the lines she'd said as she'd played the character of Maria. And she'd loved every minute of it. When she'd sung "I Feel Pretty," she had absolutely glowed with happiness. And in the end, when her onstage boyfriend Tony had died, she had cried real tears. Kiki knew she didn't have to take a part so much to heart, and she knew some people thought she got too carried away with a character, but she just couldn't help it. As far as she was concerned, acting was more than just a hobby. It was the most wonderful, exciting, important thing in the world. If you didn't live a role with every ounce of your soul, what was the point?

Kiki was sure her theory about acting was right because it worked so well for her. She was a good actress, and she knew it. Maybe she wasn't up to Barbra Streisand's level yet, but the local paper had given her a glowing review for her role as Maria, and on opening night she had actually received a standing ovation.

But even more thrilling, a famous playwright had told her she was good! Robert Marcus had three off-Broadway plays and a couple of Hollywood screenplays to his credit. He had been one of the judges for the state drama competition and had seen Kiki play Maria at the finals. Kiki had been disappointed when O. Henry hadn't won the contest, but her spirits soared when

Mr. Marcus came backstage to talk to her afterward. "You've got talent," he told her, his words sparking tingles up and down Kiki's spine. "If you keep at it and work hard, I think you could really go places."

"You mean," Kiki stammered, hardly daring to say it, "I—I could be a star?"

Kiki remembered Mr. Marcus's hearty laugh, and even now her cheeks flushed pink. She'd felt like a fool. He's just being polite, she'd told herself. I'll never be that good.

But then Mr. Marcus had met her gaze and smiled. "Yes," he said earnestly. "You've got something special. If you want it badly enough, I think perhaps someday you *could* be a star."

Now, lying on her bed, Kiki felt a shiver of excitement flash through her. "A star!" she whispered. Just saying the word made her heart beat faster.

"Kiki!" Her mother's voice broke into her memories, making her jump.

"Yes, Mama?" Kiki called back.

"Come down here to the deli and lend a hand, will you, please? Your papa's making a delivery, and I need your help."

With a sigh, Kiki pushed Oz off her stomach and got up for the second time. Hurrying down the narrow hall, she could hear the mingled voices of the customers. If only it were the sound of an eager audience instead, an audience awaiting its favorite star—Kiki Wykowski.

Suddenly, the worn wooden floors were transformed into polished marble. Kiki imagined a glittering Hollywood theater instead of her shabby Connecticut home. She was at the Academy Awards—and she'd just been named Best Actress! As she pictured herself gliding down the aisle to accept her award, her beat-up old loafers were magically converted into a pair of shiny silver high heels. Her jeans and pink cotton sweater were replaced by a slinky black evening gown. Her dark brown hair was smoothed into a perfect, elegant chignon. She walked grandly down the stairs, beginning her acceptance speech. "Ladies and gentlemen," she said, "members of the Academy, beloved fans . . ."

Kiki stepped into the deli to find her mother and at least five customers all staring at her. Instantly, her fantasy dissolved into embarrassment. The black evening gown and silver high heels disappeared, and there she was—plain old Kiki Wykowski, high-school student from Connecticut, who'd been caught mumbling to herself. Boy, did she feel silly.

"What was that all about?" Mrs. Wykowski asked, pushing a loose strand of hair out of her eyes as she dished out a helping of potato salad.

"Nothing, Mama," Kiki muttered. "Who's next?"

"Me," called a man on the other side of the counter. "I want a pastrami on rye, hold the mustard."

Kiki hurried to make up the man's order, slicing the meat, wrapping a couple of pickles, and ringing up the sale on the rickety old cash register. While she worked, she glanced over at her mother. Mrs. Wykowski's hair was hanging in her eyes, the tail of her blouse had come out of her skirt, and her forehead was creased with worry lines.

Poor Mama! Kiki thought. She looks so frazzled. Seeing her mother like that gave Kiki a familiar pang of guilt. Her parents always worked so hard, sacrificing so their children would have everything they needed.

So why can't I be satisfied with what I have? Kiki asked herself. I've got a nice home, loving parents, good friends, even a terrific boyfriend . . .

Still, life in Westdale seemed so dull. Just like in her relationship with Steve, the excitement and the magic were missing. All she could think about was Hollywood. She pictured palm trees, swimming pools, Beverly Hills mansions, and, of course, movie studios and movie stars. Lost in her daydreams once again, Kiki kept working, her imagination taking her far away from the sharp smell of mustard and the clacking of the bread slicer.

At last the lunchtime rush ended and the store emptied out. Mrs. Wykowski wiped the counter as Kiki sliced some salami and made herself a sandwich. "You know, Mama," Kiki said, taking a bite, "you ought to think about hiring someone to help out during lunchtime. I'm happy to do it when I'm around, but that's only Saturdays and Sundays. I can't imagine how you handle the crowd during the rest of the week."

"Oh, your papa and I manage." Mrs. Wykowski threw the sponge in the sink and smiled warmly at her daughter. "Someday we'll hire an extra helper. But not now. Not until we've saved enough money to make sure you and your sisters can go to college."

"But Mama," Kiki began, "I just hate to see you so worn out . . ."

Mrs. Wykowski laughed. "Me? I'm fine. I don't mind working so hard, as long as it's for a good cause. And sending my three children to college is the best cause I can think of."

Kiki bit her lip and stared down silently at her lunch. She didn't know what to say. For months she'd been trying to tell her parents the truth—that she wasn't sure she *wanted* to go to college. After all, almost none of the famous actresses of the past had gone beyond high school. Look at Molly Ringwald. She wasn't in college. She was too busy making hit movies in Hollywood for that. She was too busy being a star!

Kiki swallowed a piece of her sandwich. How can I make Mama and Papa understand? she wondered hopelessly. Her parents didn't have the same kinds of dreams she did. They'd both been born in Poland at the beginning of World War II. They'd spent their childhoods in a poor, war-torn country. Neither of them had ever had much money, neither had gone to college, and they felt like they'd missed out on a lot of great chances because of that. "You were born in the land of opportunity," Mr. Wykowski always told his daughters. "You won't have to go to work right out of junior high school, the way I did. I want you girls to go to college, get an education, and find a good job. That's why your mother and I came to America. To give our children the things we never had."

As she remembered her father's words, Kiki's food caught in her throat. Her parents would be crushed when they found out she didn't want to go to college. But Kiki knew she had to tell them. She coughed nervously, trying to figure out a way to break the news gently.

"Maybe I won't need so much money for college," she said softly. She pushed her sandwich away from her. "And you really do need help with the store right now. Don't forget, Mama, rehearsals for *The Pirates of Penzance* begin next week. I'll be staying late at school almost every afternoon. Don't you think you should get some part-time help, just until rehearsals end?"

"You've been in plays before and we've always managed," Mama answered. "What I care about is your schoolwork. Rehearsals or no rehearsals, I want you to keep your grades up."

Typical, thought Kiki. Mama and Papa just don't take my acting seriously. To them, it's just another extracurricular activity to list on my college applications. She twirled a lock of chocolate brown hair around her index finger and frowned. Why don't I just tell Mama the truth? Schoolwork doesn't matter all that much to me. It's acting that really counts.

But before Kiki could get up the nerve to open her mouth, her father walked in the back door, carrying a stack of envelopes. "The mail," he announced with a broad smile. "And look what came, Kiki. Two college catalogues." He pulled his glasses out of his shirt pocket and slipped them onto the bridge of his nose. "One from Dartmouth and one from Yale."

Mrs. Wykowski nodded approvingly. "Both very good schools."

"But, Papa," Kiki protested, "I didn't send for those."

"No, no," replied Papa, "I sent for them. And a lot of others. We'll look them over together and pick out the best ones."

Now, Kiki told herself. This is the moment to tell Mama and Papa I don't want to go to college. After graduation I'm moving to Hollywood and becoming a professional actress. But when she looked at her parents' eager faces, she knew she couldn't say it, at least not right now. Someday she'd tell them. Someday soon. But for the moment, she could only mutter, "Ivy League schools are awfully expensive."

"Don't worry about that," Mrs. Wykowski said. Her tired, red-rimmed eyes shone with happiness. "You just concentrate on getting the grades. We'll worry about the money."

Tears stung Kiki's eyes, and she turned away. She felt so frustrated! All I want to do is act, she thought miserably. There's nothing wrong with that. She pursed her lips to hold back the tears. Then why do I feel so guilty?

11

"Is something wrong, Kiki?" her mother asked with concern.

Quickly, Kiki wiped her eyes and shook her head. "It's the sandwich," she lied. "I put too much hot mustard on it." She forced herself to smile. "Whew, I forgot how hot that stuff is!"

She couldn't let her parents down. They'd be so disappointed. After they'd worked so hard, given up so much on account of her.

"Thanks, Papa," she said. "I'll look them over. I really appreciate it."

Kiki pasted on a bright smile and tucked the catalogues under her arm before heading back up to her room.

Her best performance, but she would never win an Academy Award for it. Instead, she would be trading stardom for boredom, fame and fortune for blackboards and blue books.

Kiki swallowed hard against the lump of rye bread stuck in her throat that just wouldn't go down.

Chapter Two

KIKI THREW OPEN HER CLOSET DOOR AND let her gaze wander over the row of dresses. "Now, what should I wear for my date with Steve," she muttered to herself. Perhaps something old-fashioned and romantic, like the lacy, high-collared blouse she'd found last month in the local thrift shop, Secondhand Rose. Or what about an outfit a little more elegant, like the silky, pale pink dress she'd bought for last year's Valentine's Day dance? She giggled. Maybe she'd shock Steve and go punk—lots of eye makeup, a sleeveless black T-shirt decorated with safety pins, a dozen plastic bracelets on each wrist . . .

But then she turned away from the closet and frowned. Why bother? she thought irritably. She and Steve were going to do exactly what they did every Saturday night—catch a movie at the Nickelodeon Theater, then head over to the local ice-cream parlor for a sundae. What was the point of dressing up for that?

As Kiki reached for a simple, forest green sweater-dress, Oz hopped off the bed and came over to rub against her legs. The little calico kitten reminded her of just how wonderful Steve could be. Just before Christmas last year, Kiki had fallen in love with one particular kitten in the window of the local pet shop, The Cat's Miaow. So, secretly, Steve had bought it for her, delivering it bright and early on Christmas morning, complete with a big red bow around its neck. He'd even named the cat already—Oz, after Kiki's favorite movie, *The Wizard of Oz*.

"And that's not all, Oz," Kiki said, slipping into her dress, then sitting on the floor to tug on her boots. "Steve is smart, and good-looking, and kind, and steady." She frowned. "Too steady, if you want to know the truth. There just isn't any surprise or mystery left between us. You know, he's so predictable I can practically set my watch by that guy." Kiki stood up and glanced at the digital clock on her night table. It was exactly seven-thirty when the doorbell rang downstairs. Kiki gave Oz a final pat. "Steve's on time, as usual," she said with a frown.

Kiki ran downstairs and threw open the front door. Gazing into Steve's smiling face, she felt a pang of guilt. He's a wonderful guy, she told herself, and I shouldn't put him down. To make up for it, she pulled him close and gave him a warm kiss.

"Well," Steve laughed, "what did I do to deserve that?"

"Nothing," Kiki replied, vaguely annoyed that Steve was reacting so calmly. Just once she

14

wished he'd do something really wild and romantic. Maybe pick her up and carry her away with him, like Richard Gere did to Debra Winger at the end of *An Officer and a Gentleman*. But then, that wasn't Steve's style.

"Hello, Steve," Mr. Wykowski said, walking in from the kitchen. "Where are you two off to tonight?"

"Hi, Mr. Wykowski," Steve said. "We're going to the Nickelodeon to see *Flashdance*. We've both seen it before, but Kiki wants to see it again."

Steve and Mr. Wykowski began chatting about the first big snowstorm of the year that had recently hit Westdale. Kiki listened with one ear, staring absently at the walnut sideboard in the foyer. On it were the two college catalogues that had come in the mail earlier in the afternoon. Seeing them, she could hardly wait to get out of the house. If Papa makes me look through those dumb catalogues with him, I think I'll go nuts, she thought glumly. She grabbed her red winter coat and plaid scarf and reached for the doorknob. "Let's go, Steve," she said impatiently. "I don't want to miss the coming attractions."

A minute later, they were shuffling through the snow to Steve's car, a beat-up Jeep Cherokee he shared with his older brother. "You seemed kind of eager to get out of there," he said as he put the Jeep in gear and started down the street.

"I was." Kiki turned to Steve. "Remember I

15

told you Papa sent away for all those college catalogues? Well, now Mama's on my case about choosing a school, too." She pushed her dark brown hair back from her forehead and sighed. "What am I going to do, Steve? My parents have college on the brain. How am I going to tell them I want to skip school and be an actress instead?"

"But why does it have to be one or the other?" Steve asked. "Lots of schools have good drama departments. Why can't you study acting and make your parents happy at the same time?"

Kiki sucked in her breath, annoyed. "Acting isn't the kind of thing you learn in school," she said. "The only way to become famous is to get out there and *make movies!* I mean, look at John Travolta. He didn't even finish high school, and he's one of the biggest stars in the world."

"Maybe so, but that's very rare. You can't count on the same thing happening to you. Just think, Kiki, you've acted in only three or four high-school plays. If you went to college you'd get a lot more experience. You could take acting classes, and get involved in college shows, and—"

"But I don't have time for that," Kiki interrupted. "Judy Garland was starring in *The Wizard of Oz* when she was my age. I want to be famous *now.*"

"Look," said Steve, turning the Jeep onto Main Street. He drove past the bank and the Westdale post office. "If you want to be an actress, I think that's great. But all you talk about is becoming a star. And you want it to happen overnight." He shrugged. "Well, I just don't think it works that way. First you have to study hard, and do a lot of small productions before you're ready for the big time. Becoming famous doesn't happen by magic. If you're not realistic about this whole thing, you'll just be disappointed."

"Oh, yeah? Since when do *you* know so much about it?" Kiki challenged. Steve loved acting in school plays—in fact, he and Kiki had met in last year's production of *Guys and Dolls*—but theater was only a hobby for him. He wasn't passionate about it the way Kiki was. As for a career, he wanted to be a veterinarian. He'd known that ever since he was a little kid.

"I'm no authority," Steve answered reasonably. "I'm just telling you what I've read."

Kiki let out an exasperated sigh. Lately, Steve was beginning to drive her just a little crazy. And the funny thing was, the exact same things that had attracted her to him in the first place were the things that annoyed her now.

From the first time she'd met him during the *Guys and Dolls* production, Kiki had been attracted to Steve's easygoing manner and good humor. He had a way of smoothing over every crisis that popped up. If someone's costume split a seam, he'd calmly find a needle and thread and sew it up. If the lead in the musical suddenly came down with a massive case of laryngitis, he'd make all the arrangements for a

17

replacement before anyone had a chance to panic. Steve was great at turning mountains back into molehills.

But sometimes Kiki didn't want to be calmed down. As far as she was concerned, her acting career *was* a mountain, and she didn't want Steve turning it into an insignificant molehill by warning her that her dreams might not come true.

Steve drove around the snow-covered town green and turned onto Court Street. He pulled the Jeep into a parking space and turned off the engine. "Well, here we are," he said with a smile.

Kiki felt like screaming. How can Steve be so calm and rational all the time? she wondered irritably. If he were a scientist, she told herself, he would have insisted that the big-bang theory for the earth's creation was all bunk. Because Steve almost never did anything in a big way. He'd rather let things evolve little by little. He never took chances. And for someone as adventurous as Kiki, it was infuriating. Her theory was that if you never went out on a limb, you'd never get to the top of the tree.

Kiki hopped out of the Jeep and started up the sidewalk toward the movie theater. Steve fell into step beside her and took her hand. As they walked along, she glanced over at him, trying to view him not as Steve Goldman, her boy-friend of a year and a half, but as a stranger—someone she was seeing for the first time. He was handsome, no doubt about that. Tall and well-built, with regular features, beautiful wavy blond hair, and large green eyes. But he was hardly what you'd call sophisticated-looking or chic. Tonight he was wearing his usual outfit—Frye boots, cords, a flannel shirt, and a blue ski jacket. His hair was mussed, and, as usual, his pants were covered with short yellow hairs from his golden retriever, Amos.

Steve is a real country boy, Kiki thought. He liked hiking and camping, riding horses, and ice-skating on Silverwood Lake. He was kind and funny and friendly . . . but no way could Kiki imagine him in Hollywood. She smiled ruefully, trying to picture him behind the wheel of a Porsche or a Jaguar. The image just didn't work. Good old dependable Steve, with his realistic, down-to-earth attitude, didn't fit into Kiki's idea of the wild parties and flashy discos frequented by the Beverly Hills glitter crowd.

Kiki and Steve stepped into the Nickelodeon Theater, and Steve shrugged out of his plain blue down jacket. For an instant, Kiki pictured him in a black tuxedo and a silk bow tie, but the image was gone just as fast.

"Hey, far-out, it's Kiki and Steve," someone called. Kiki turned around to find her friend, Lou Greenspan, and Lou's boyfriend, Ethan Kramer. Lou and Ethan were both wild about the sixties, and they liked to dress the part. Tonight, Lou was wearing an oversize army jacket and a tricornered hat with a No Nukes button pinned to the side. Ethan was in his usual jeans

19

and oxford-cloth shirt, but he had a thin string of love beads around his neck.

"Hi, guys," Steve said. "Ready to watch Jennifer Beals do her thing?"

"You bet," replied Ethan. "If I weren't so into Lou, here, I'd go look up Jennifer," he teased.

"Funny, Ethan," Lou said sarcastically, "but I'm not laughing, and I don't think Jennifer would be, either." She adjusted her hat.

Kiki giggled. "Hey, Lou," she said, "that hat is great. It looks like it could have come straight out of the Revolutionary War." She peered more closely at it and noticed a small, black-rimmed hole in one side. "Gosh, where'd you get it? That looks like a real bullet hole!"

"Oh, no," Lou said quickly, "your imagination must be working overtime." She took the hat off and looked at it. When she saw the hole, she laughed uncomfortably. "I got it at . . . at Secondhand Rose. It's probably just a moth hole." She shrugged and put the hat back on. Then she smiled nervously at Kiki.

Kiki frowned. Lately, Lou acted as if she were hiding something a lot of the time. Kiki couldn't put her finger on just what—but she was close enough with Lou to know when something was up. Lou was definitely not a good liar.

"Let's go get seats before the theater fills up too much," Lou said, changing the subject.

While Steve and Ethan got tickets, Kiki and Lou bought two large cartons of popcorn and four sodas. As Kiki dug into the pocket of her dress for money, Lou cried, "Hey, there's Ashley and Len!'' She pointed to her computer-whiz friend, Ashley Calhoun, and her boyfriend.

Kiki waved casually to her friend.

"Hold on a sec, Kiki,'' Lou continued. "I've got to talk to Ash.'' She dashed over to the other girl, pulled her into a corner of the theater's lobby and began talking in an excited whisper.

Kiki frowned. Those two have been acting awfully strange these days, she told herself. I wonder what's going on.

Ethan and Steve came back with the tickets, and the three of them went into the theater to find seats. A moment later, Lou joined them.

"What was all that with Ashley about?'' Kiki asked.

"Oh . . . nothing,'' Lou hedged.

Kiki didn't have the chance to question her friend further because the lights dimmed and suddenly the huge white screen was a splash of Technicolor. Kiki slid down in her seat and leaned her head against Steve's shoulder.

The magic was beginning once again. As the coming attractions took form on the screen, Kiki felt like she was slowly being pulled to a faraway place. If Movieland were a real live country, then previews were the plane ride to it. In that strange, wonderful place, Lou and Ashley's mysterious secret no longer mattered, nor did Kiki's problems with her parents and college or her annoyance with Steve. She adored the feeling of sitting in a dark movie theater, chomping on popcorn and watching characters and stories

21

come alive. Sometimes she didn't even care what movie she was seeing.

The opening credits of *Flashdance* rolled down the screen, and soon Jennifer was performing her heart out. Kiki was there right alongside of her. Watching the film for the second time, Kiki decided that the story line was like her own life. Pouring your heart and soul into something, even though everyone else says it's impossible.

By the time the movie was over, Kiki was wrapped in euphoria and could barely keep from dancing her way up the aisle. Steve took her hand and they started toward the exit.

"You know, I heard Jennifer Beals was a straight A student at Yale," Steve remarked.

Suddenly, Kiki came crashing back to earth. College! Couldn't Steve think of anything else? He was beginning to sound exactly like her father! Kiki wriggled her hand out of Steve's grasp. "Look, I know acting is risky," she said with annoyance, "but I have to take the plunge sometime. The sooner I get serious about my career, the sooner I'll find out if I have what it takes."

"I know how you feel, Kiki," Steve replied in a maddeningly reasonable voice. "But I still think college is a good idea. That way, if acting doesn't work out—or if you decide you don't really want to be an actress after all—you'll have something to fall back on."

"How could I ever not want to be an actress?" Kiki exclaimed. That was just the kind of thinking her parents would come up with.

No matter how many times she told them she loved acting, they refused to see it as anything but a hobby. And now Steve was behaving exactly the same way.

What I need is to get away, Kiki told herself. Far away. Away from the deli. From Mama and Papa. And from small-town thinkers like Steve. All I want is to just get on a bus heading west, all the way to Hollywood . . .

"Wanna head over to the ice-cream shop with Lou and Ethan for a sundae?" Steve asked as they walked out onto the cold, snow-covered street.

Kiki pursed her lips. Steve Goldman, she said to herself, you are as predictable as a Swiss watch. In a flash of stubbornness, she turned and stared at Steve, her head tilted defiantly to one side. "No, thanks," she said. "I think I'll just go home."

Steve looked at her uncertainly. "But—"

"I've got a headache," Kiki lied. "And besides, I . . . I'm just not hungry."

Kiki knew her excuse was pretty feeble, but Steve didn't protest. His expression tightened, then he turned and started down the sidewalk to the Jeep. Somehow, that made Kiki even madder. I'm lying and he knows it, she thought irritably. Why doesn't he yell at me? Why does he always have to be so nice?

Kiki pulled her coat around her as a chilling wind made her shiver. She felt a lump rise in her throat. What became of the excitement Steve and I used to have together? she wondered sadly. Back in the beginning, everything we did seemed thrilling—even just watching a movie or playing with Amos in Steve's backyard. Lately, though, our dates have all the zing and excitement of Velveeta cheese.

She frowned and glanced over at Steve. He was standing by the Jeep, staring down at the sidewalk and kicking the snow with his boots. Looking at his handsome profile, she felt a rush of emotion wash over her. I still love him, she realized. So why do I feel so confused?

Impulsively, Kiki hurried over to him and slipped her arm through his. It's not Steve's fault, really, she thought. He just doesn't understand about my acting. Maybe he'll never understand. "You know," she said, "I think I would like that sundae after all."

Steve's handsome face broke into a smile. "Great," he cried, opening the Jeep door for her. He bowed dramatically. "Your limo awaits, mademoiselle."

Kiki got in and let out a ragged sigh. If only it *were* a limo, she thought wistfully. Closing her eyes, she drifted into her favorite daydream. The beat-up Jeep became a stretch limo with tinted windows, Steve turned into Hollywood's most popular male star, and Kiki could hear the swish of her silk dress and the popping of champagne corks . . .

Chapter Three

"WHY, KIKI, DAH-LING, IT'S BEEN AGES!"

Kiki turned from her locker to see Ramona De Salvo hurrying down the hall. Her black hair bounced around her shoulders, and her large dark eyes shone. In her embroidered Mexican shirt, white blouse, and silver earrings, she looked almost like a senorita from old Mexico, waiting to throw a rose to her favorite bullfighter. But upon closer inspection, the modern American side of Ramona was visible—there was a mint green Swatch watch strapped to her wrist, a backpack slung over her shoulder, and on her feet she wore a pair of red ankle boots.

"Ramona, sweetheart!" Kiki cried, grabbing her friend and kissing her on both cheeks. "Didn't I see you at the Academy Awards last week?"

Ramona let out a weary sigh. "Oh, yes. It's such a bore, but when you're nominated for five Oscars, well, what can you do? I just couldn't disappoint my fans."

"I know just what you mean," Kiki said with a savvy nod. "After your tenth or eleventh time at those ceremonies, they kind of lose their zing."

She tried to keep a straight face, but finally she and Ramona burst into hysterical giggles.

The two girls adored acting out characters. They'd been doing it together ever since they'd first become friends. They could be totally silly, like when they pretended they were world-weary movie stars, but their little game had come in handy a few times too, like when they'd gotten backstage at the Stevie Nicks concert by convincing the bouncers they were her cousins.

Ramona brushed a strand of jet black hair away from her eyes. "Are you getting a ride home with Steve today?" she asked.

"No, he's working on a history project with Jordan Zimmerman and Alicia Sanchez."

"Alicia Sanchez!" Ramona raised an eyebrow. "If I were you, I'd get up to the library and keep an eye on that boyfriend of yours. Knowing Alicia, she'll probably lure him into the stacks and seduce him."

Kiki laughed. Alicia was famous around O. Henry High for her slow curves and fast reputation. "I'm not worried. Steve is as steady as the Rock of Gibraltar." She rolled her chocolate brown eyes skyward and added, "Unfortunately."

Ramona frowned. "Unfortunately? What do you mean?"

"Oh, I don't know. I guess Steve and I have been seeing each other for so long that"—Kiki searched for the right words—"he's lost his zing for me—just like those Academy Awards we were talking about." She smiled weakly. "Steve's so laid back sometimes I feel like checking his pulse to make sure he's still breathing!"

Ramona looked closely at her friend. "Hey, this sounds serious."

Kiki shrugged. "No, it's nothing really. It's just . . . Oh, I don't know."

"Well, if you ever need someone to talk to about it, you know I'm here." Ramona linked her arm through Kiki's. "Anyway, I was just on my way over to Secondhand Rose to look for costumes for *The Pirates of Penzance.* Why don't you come, too?"

"Sounds great," Kiki exclaimed. She smiled gratefully at her friend's support. The girls were two of a kind—even down to the fact that Ramona was Kiki's understudy for the lead in O. Henry High's upcoming production of *The Pirates of Penzance,* in addition to being the costume designer.

The two friends shared a love of excitement and adventure, and they were both looking for something more than the route their parents expected them to take after high school. Ramona's mother assumed she was going to go to college just like her three older brothers. But Ramona dreamed of traveling, the same way Kiki dreamed about Hollywood. Just like Kiki, Ramona was looking for something thrilling in life . . . the only difference was that Ramona wasn't sure how exactly she was going to get her thrills. She talked about everything from driving a truck to scuba diving for Jacques Cousteau to running for governor.

"I think a little costume-hunting would be just the thing to pick up my mood," Kiki told her friend. "Let me get a couple of books, and then we'll hit Secondhand Rose."

"Super. I could use another opinion before I buy anything." As Kiki pulled a few reading assignments out of her locker, Ramona slipped into her navy down jacket.

Half an hour and a short bus ride later, the girls were rummaging through piles of shirts at their favorite thrift store. The wooden bins, filled to overflowing, held a promising assortment of mismatched clothing. A flapper dress from the 1920s was mixed in with a felt poodle skirt from the fifties and a pair of tie-dyed bell-bottoms from the sixties. Hats, gloves, ties, shoes—you name it, you could find it at Secondhand Rose.

"Oh, boy," said Ramona eagerly. "It looks like they just got a lot of new stuff. We should be able to find some fantastic costumes here." She rooted through the nearest bin and came up with a battered army cap. Putting it on, she gave Kiki a crisp salute and said, "Captain Ramona De Salvo reporting for duty."

"At ease, Captain," Kiki said with a laugh. She picked up a worn jean-jacket that had a peace sign embroidered with rainbow-colored thread on the back. "Wow, Lou would die if she saw this," Kiki exclaimed. "It's got to be vintage sixties." She turned over the price tag thoughtfully. "It's only seven dollars. Maybe I'll buy it for her as a present."

"She'll love you forever," Ramona said with a laugh.

But then Kiki frowned. "But you know, I'm

28

kind of mad at Lou right now. She's been acting awfully strange lately. It's as though she's always got some big secret. Like last weekend when I saw her at the Nickelodeon, she and Ashley just couldn't wait to run off together and whisper. Made me feel kind of left out.''

Ramona nodded, pulling the army cap off her head and dropping it back into the bin. ''I know what you mean. But it's not just Lou and Ashley. Tina's been really weird, too. Like last week I saw her reading this really old copy of *The Adventures of Huckleberry Finn*—leather binding and everything. But when I asked her where she got it, she clammed up.''

Kiki pursed her lips. ''Those three are supposed to be our closest friends,'' she said. ''If there's a secret, I want to know about it.''

''Me, too,'' Ramona agreed. ''Besides, I'm getting kind of worried about Ashley. Every time I see her, she's got a stack of history books in her arms.'' She shook her head. ''Anyone who'd study that hard for Mrs. Killington's class has got to be seriously ill!''

Kiki laughed. ''Well, I say it's time to confront those guys and find out what's going on.'' She tucked the jean-jacket under her arm, then continued rummaging through one of the bins of clothing.

''Right. After all, what if there's something really wrong? Maybe we can help.''

''For sure,'' Kiki said. ''Okay, so let's corner them in school tomorrow and force the truth out.'' She discarded a few old skirts and polyester shirts,

29

digging into the bottom of the pile of clothes. Suddenly she noticed a piece of silky yellow material peeking out from under a heap of matchless socks. Pushing the socks aside, she pulled out a crumpled yellow garment and shook it out. It unfolded into a dress—a beautiful ankle-length dress with a low bodice and short, puffy sleeves. "Oh, Ramona," she cried, "look at this! It would be perfect for *Pirates!*" She held it against her body. "What do you think?"

"You're right. Once that dress is cleaned and pressed, you'll look just like Linda Ronstadt did in the movie version of *The Pirates of Penzance.*"

"I love it," Kiki said, a happy giggle escaping from inside her. "It's a real movie-star gown!"

"Hey, how about this?" Ramona exclaimed, producing a ruffled white shirt from one of the bins. "It would be great for the pirate king!" She pulled it over her head and sighed. "That's the role for me. None of that helpless female stuff. I want danger, adventure . . ." She dropped into a fencing stance and shouted, *"En garde!"*

"Oh, save me!" Kiki cried, clasping her hands in front of her. "Please!"

"I will show no mercy!" Ramona growled, carving the air with her imaginary sword.

The girls collapsed into giggles.

"I can't wait to show these things to the rest of the cast," Ramona said.

"Really," agreed Kiki.

"Come on," Ramona said, grabbing her friend's arm. "Let's pay and get out of here.

Bob's coming over for dinner tonight, and I want to get home before he shows up.''

Kiki walked over to the checkout counter, cradling the yellow dress and the beat-up 1960s' jean-jacket. Ramona and Bob seemed like the perfect couple—always together, always holding hands and whispering deliciously sappy, romantic things to each other. That's how it used to be with Steve and me, Kiki thought. So what's changed? Not Steve. He's still as loving and caring as always. It's me, she realized. I finally figured out once and for all that I don't belong in Westdale.

Steve's a wonderful guy, but I was meant for bigger things, Kiki thought as she paid the cashier for her purchase. I was meant for Hollywood.

Kiki couldn't believe it. For the tenth time since history class had begun, Ashley raised her hand.

Mrs. Killington gave a stiff little frown. ''Yes, Miss Calhoun, what is it now?'' Her glasses slipped farther down her nose as she peered disapprovingly at Ashley. With her gray hair sprayed in the stiff shape of a helmet, she resembled a general leading her troops into battle.

''Uh, it just seems to me that historians have got Cleopatra all wrong,'' Ashley said.

''Oh?'' Mrs. Killington replied. ''How so?''

''Well, it wasn't really her fault all those men fell in love with her. I mean, when she first met Marc Antony, she thought he was a total nerd!''

The class burst out laughing. Kiki turned to Ramona and whispered, ''Boy, the way she talks, you'd think she actually knew Cleopatra personally!"

"At least she's more interesting to listen to than 'Killer' Killington," Ramona replied. "That woman is like a shot of novocaine!"

"Yeah, but Ashley's sudden interest in the past just doesn't make sense." Kiki frowned. "She's into computers, not history."

Charmaine Parker leaned across the aisle to comment: "I think Ashley has developed ESP. Either that, or her body has been taken over by a spirit from beyond the grave." Her huge green eyes wore their usual dreamy expression. Dressed in a Victorian blouse from her mother's antique shop and a skirt made from an old patchwork quilt, with her chestnut curls flowing past her shoulders, Charmaine resembled a girl from another era herself.

Kiki stifled a giggle. She knew Charmaine was perfectly serious. Her friend was crazy about astrology, spiritualism, Ouija boards—anything that had to do with the unknown. "All I know," Kiki whispered back, "is that Ashley, Tina, and Lou have all been really weird lately."

"You noticed, too?" Charmaine asked, her green eyes flashing.

"You bet," Ramona whispered. "I think we should talk to Ashley right after class."

"Me, too," Charmaine replied. "If Ashley needs an evil spirit exorcised, we've got to stick with her and give her all the help we can. Besides, I've got a book of spells that I think might work."

Mrs. Killington's class ticked away even more

slowly than usual. The moment the bell rang, Kiki, Ramona, and Charmaine jumped up and surrounded Ashley, moving her purposely toward the hallway.

"Okay, Cleopatra, we've got some questions for you to answer," Kiki said.

"Hey, what's going on?" Ashley asked, confused.

"That's what *we* want to know," Ramona demanded. She pushed open the door, and the girls piled out of the classroom and into the crowded corridor.

Ashley shook her shaggy red hair out of her eyes and nibbled nervously on the nail of one slender finger. "I—I don't know what you're talking about," she insisted.

"Oh yeah?" Kiki said. "Then let me explain. Every time I see you and Lou and Tina together, you're huddled in a corner whispering like crazy. Something's up, that's obvious. Now what is it?"

"Um," Ashley stalled, her brown eyes darting around the hallway.

"Since when are you so into history?" Ramona asked. "Lately, it's like you've been competing with Killington for the history prize of the month."

"Yeah," Kiki agreed, "history used to be your worst subject. Seems to me you were barely squeaking by with a seventy-eight average last marking period. Now you're the class expert."

"How do you know so much about ancient Egypt?" Charmaine put in.

Ashley shrugged, trying to seem nonchalant.

33

"I've been reading a few books, that's all. It's a fascinating subject."

"Yeah, but in class today you were talking as if you'd actually been there," Ramona pursued. "I mean, how did you know Egyptian sandals were made out of goathide rather than cowhide?"

"Well, I—"

"Come on, Ashley," Charmaine insisted. "We know something's wrong, and we want to help. Just tell us when you first felt the spirit enter your body."

"Huh?" Ashley said with alarm.

"Never mind her," Kiki interrupted. "Look, Ashley, we're your friends. If you're in trouble, we want to help."

"It's not that. It's just, well . . ." Ashley bit her lip nervously. "It's a secret," she said finally, giving a weak shrug.

"Come on, you can tell us," Ramona urged. "We're your best friends, right?"

"Of course," agreed Ashley, "but this just isn't the sort of thing I can go blabbing around the whole school."

"But we're not the whole school," Charmaine insisted. "Besides, Lou and Tina know, right?"

Ashley hesitated. "Well . . . yes. But they're the only ones." She frowned. "So far, everything's worked out fine, but if too many people find out, there could be serious trouble."

"Listen, if you can't trust us," Kiki said, "who *can* you trust?" She wrapped a comforting arm around Ashley. "Remember when you made me promise not to tell anyone about the

34

big crush you had on Len Cassinerio? Well, I kept the secret, didn't I?''

''Besides,'' added Ramona, ''if this thing's really so serious, then you shouldn't keep it to yourself. Who knows? You might need our help.''

''Oh, come on,'' moaned Charmaine. ''The suspense is killing us!''

Ashley looked at her friends with a serious expression. For a long moment, she didn't say anything. Then finally she sighed. ''Well . . . all right. But you have to swear you'll never tell a living soul!''

''We swear!'' the three other girls cried together. Kiki leaned closer. ''What's the big news?''

But Ashley just shook her head. ''I can't tell you here. Come over to my house right after school, and I'll show you. You wouldn't believe it unless you saw it for yourselves anyway.''

Kiki caught her breath. She was so curious she could barely stand it. But she had a *Pirates of Penzance* rehearsal that afternoon. For a second she almost considered skipping it. But acting was too important—even more important than Ashley's tempting secret. Besides, Ramona had to go to the rehearsal, too. They'd just have to meet Ashley later in the afternoon.

''We should be done with the *Pirates* run-through by five-thirty,'' Kiki said. ''Suppose we hit your place around six?''

''Okay,'' Ashley nodded. ''And prepare to be amazed,'' she added with a meaningful glance. ''What you see this afternoon is going to change your whole life!''

Chapter Four

KIKI STUFFED HER *PIRATES OF PENZANCE* script into her bag, pulled on her red coat, and hurried out to the school parking lot to meet Steve. "Thanks for picking me up," she said as she joined him. They started walking slowly toward the old wishing well behind the school, the snow crunching softly beneath their feet.

"Anytime." Steve smiled and leaned close to give Kiki a kiss. "How'd the rehearsal go this afternoon?"

"Okay. But some of the pirates can barely carry a tune. I wish you'd tried out. I know you would have gotten a part."

"I wanted to, but I really don't have time for a school play right now. If I don't ace every one of my science courses, I'll never make it into a good pre-vet program."

Kiki didn't answer. She admired Steve's persistence and devotion, but sometimes it all seemed so dull. He had been a top student all through high school. After graduation, he'd just have to keep it up for another five years and eventually he'd be a vet. It was hard, but it was also so predictable. Acting just wasn't that way. It took the same hard work and persistence, but it also involved talent, and passion, and a lot of luck. To Kiki, becoming a vet was like plodding up a steep hill. Acting was standing on the edge of a cliff and leaping off into the unknown.

"So what'll it be tonight?" Steve asked as they stepped into the secluded glade of trees which surrounded the well. "Chinese food or Mexican?" He smiled. "You know, it's great being with someone who likes spicy food as much as I do. You're the only girl I've ever met who can eat a whole jalapeño pepper without smoke coming out of her ears."

Kiki coughed uncomfortably. "I, uh, wanted to talk to you about our dinner date, Steve. I, um, well, I have to cancel it."

Kiki watched as a pained, unhappy expression clouded Steve's face. She suddenly felt horrible. Steve really cared about her, and she was hurting him.

Kiki's first impulse was to tell Steve the truth—that tonight she was going to learn Ashley's mysterious secret. But she knew Ashley would kill her if she mentioned even that much, so she thought fast to come up with a plausible excuse.

"Um, Ashley and I are working on an extra-credit project for English. Mrs. Shafer just assigned it today, and it's due next week."

"Oh," Steve said. "Well, we'll have to go out another night. Hey, listen, my folks are renting a Gene Kelly movie this weekend, so we should get together and watch it." He walked over to

37

the well, leaning against its mossy old stones. "It's one of your favorites—*Singin' in the Rain*."

Kiki ran a mittened hand along the top of the well. Flakes of snow fell into the dark, half-frozen water. "Sounds good." She looked up at Steve and smiled. But it didn't quite mute the note of tension that seemed to follow them everywhere these days.

Steve smiled back and, slipping his arm around her waist, pulled her toward him. He leaned forward, his lips meeting hers in a soft, warm kiss. He held her for a quiet moment. "Shall we make a wish?" he said finally. He produced two pennies from his pocket and handed one to her. Steve did have the marvelous ability to smooth over uncomfortable moments. It was just sad that they'd been having so many of those moments lately. Kiki reached for his hand and gave it a warm squeeze. Together, they leaned over the well and gazed into the darkness.

But at the moment that Kiki dropped the penny into the water, her mind was far, far away from Steve, O. Henry High, and Westdale, Connecticut. *Please*, she wished, silently mouthing the words, *make me a star*. The coin fell into the icy water with a plop. A second later, Steve's penny joined it.

Kiki looked up, staring into the darkening sky. A sliver of moon was resting on its back, surrounded by a few sparkling stars. My name's going to sparkle just like that, she thought, when it's lit by dozens of tiny light bulbs on a Hollywood theater marquee. Kiki pictured herself

38

waiting backstage at "The Tonight Show." "And now," Johnny Carson was saying, "one of America's newest stars, Kiki Wykowski!"

"I guess your wish wasn't quite the same as the one you made on our first date."

"Huh?" Kiki turned her thoughts back to Westdale and Steve. "What do you mean?"

"Remember," Steve said slowly, "you told me later that you'd wished I'd fall in love with you. Well, I can guess from that faraway look in your eyes that tonight's wish had nothing to do with me." He frowned. "What's happened to us, Kiki? Something's different—like we're never on the same wavelength anymore. I can feel it . . . and I know you can, too."

Kiki stared solemnly into Steve's face, shivering slightly in the cold winter evening. She didn't quite know what to say. If she told Steve nothing had changed, she'd be lying. But if she said she'd stopped loving him, that wouldn't be true, either. I'm not ready to break up with Steve, she told herself. Not until I've had a chance to sort out my feelings. Not until I'm sure.

"Look," Steve said, his voice catching. "Maybe we should stop seeing so much of each other for a little while. I mean, I have a lot of work to do on my college applications, and you're busy with *The Pirates of Penzance*. It would be a good time to cool things off for a while and see how we really feel about each other. If we really miss each other, we can get back together again. If not, well . . ." He left the last words unsaid.

A sudden, surprising pang of hurt shot

through Kiki. She could tell that Steve was trying to sound casual, but she could hear the pain in his voice. Watching him, her heart ached and she longed to throw her arms around him and kiss all the hurt away. But then she stopped herself. Steve's right, she thought. If we weren't meant to be together, it's better for us to find out now. Biting her lip, she looked out across the snowy lawn and nodded. "It's probably a good idea," she said uncertainly.

For a moment, neither one of them spoke. Then Steve took a deep breath and said, "Come on. I'll drive you over to Ashley's."

Steve headed across the glade toward the parking lot, turning his back on the wishing well where he and Kiki had first fallen in love. Following behind, Kiki felt tears welling up in her eyes. What's the matter with me? she wondered, gritting her teeth to hold back the tears. *I'm* the one who's been feeling bored. I should be glad about the chance to cool things off. This way I'll be able to figure how I really feel about Steve. And in the meantime, well, who knows? Maybe I'll even meet someone else—someone exciting, unpredictable, romantic . . .

But even her fantasies couldn't erase the dull ache she felt inside. She got into Steve's Jeep and sat there, staring out the frost-covered window, cold and miserable. As Steve drove toward Ashley's house, neither of them said a word. Steve turned the radio on and it seemed to Kiki that every sad song was meant for her. Worst of all was how uncomfortable she felt sitting next to him. Kiki and Steve had always been so relaxed together. But in just one afternoon, all that had changed. The ride seemed to take a year—a very depressing year.

When they finally pulled into Ashley's driveway, Kiki had to stop herself from turning toward Steve to kiss him good-bye. There would be no good-night kiss tonight. Not tonight, and maybe not ever.

Kiki pressed her lips together to keep from crying. I can't believe this, she said to herself, the reality of what had happened hitting her like a sharp slap. No more warm hugs on cold afternoons. No more popcorn fights over TV movies. No more Steve . . . It's what I wanted, she reminded herself. At least, I *thought* I did.

Steve stared down at the steering wheel and cleared his throat. "So long, Kiki," he said softly.

Kiki blinked against her tears. "Okay," she mumbled. "So long." Opening the door, she got out and started up the steps to Ashley's front door. Then suddenly, impulsively, she turned around, all ready to run back and tell Steve how much she loved him. But the Jeep was already pulling out of the driveway. As Kiki watched, Steve shifted into first and took off up the street, without so much as a backward glance.

It took every bit of Kiki's acting skill to smile when Ashley's mother opened the front door. "I thought I heard someone out here," she said. "Come in before you turn into an icicle."

"Thanks, Mrs. Calhoun," Kiki said, stepping

41

into the warm house and pulling off her mittens. As usual, just standing inside the Calhoun house left Kiki awestruck. She looked around at the Oriental carpets, the elegant vases and figurines on the mantelpiece, the large oil paintings of the Calhoun ancestors that lined the walls. Boy, she thought, this place is as different from my house as a caterpillar from a butterfly. But then owning a big computer plant like Ashley's father did was a heck of a lot different from owning a neighborhood delicatessen!

"Ramona and Charmaine just got here a second ago," Mrs. Calhoun said in her lilting southern accent. "They're upstairs with Ashley, along with three bags of potato chips and enough soda to float the house." She laughed lightly. "Go on up, honey. Make yourself at home."

Kiki walked up the plushly carpeted stairs, marveling at how poised and charming Mrs. Calhoun always seemed to be. She'd probably act like that even if the roof caved in around her, Kiki thought. But *me*—my boyfriend suggests we cool it for a while and I practically fall apart.

She paused outside Ashley's door and squared her shoulders. She wasn't going to let her friends see how upset she was—not now, when everyone was so excited about Ashley's secret. She knocked on the door.

Ashley threw open the door, grinning. "Kiki, hi! How was rehearsal? Ramona said you were super fantastic."

"It was okay," Kiki answered, doing her best

42

to sound cheerful and normal. She shrugged out of her coat and flopped down on Ashley's bed.

Ramona was leaning back in the chair in front of Ashley's computer, her feet propped up on the desk. "Well, now that we're all here," she said, "it's time for Ashley to spill her secret. Come on, Ash, what gives?"

"If I have to wait another minute to find out what's up, I'm going to flip a psychic circuit," Charmaine said, stretching out on the floor and munching a handful of potato chips. "I brought along some books on spirit possession, and we're going to do whatever we can to help you out."

"This has nothing to do with spirits," Ashley replied with a laugh. Then her expression grew solemn. She looked from Kiki to Ramona to Charmaine and said simply, "I've discovered a way to travel back in time."

Kiki stared at Ashley in disbelief. Travel back in time? she thought incredulously. She must be kidding! But no, Ashley looked completely serious. Kiki shook her head. Poor Ashley! She must be suffering from some kind of delusion brought on by all those hours of hitting the history books.

Ramona reacted by bursting out laughing. "This is some kind of joke, right?"

Ashley smiled. "I knew you wouldn't believe me. That's why I asked you to come over tonight. Lou is in the past right now. I sent her back while Ramona and Charmaine were coming up the stairs." She glanced quickly at her digital wristwatch. "She should be back in just a few seconds. Then you'll understand."

"Ooh!" squealed Charmaine, looking eagerly around the room. "This is so exciting! Lou, Lou, can you hear us?"

Oh, no, thought Kiki. Don't tell me Charmaine actually believes her! But then, Charmaine accepted a lot of theories that Kiki thought were more than a little off-the-wall. Only someone who was absolutely positive that she could commune with George Washington through a Ouija board would swallow something like this!

"Don't worry, Ashley," Kiki said earnestly. "You've just been working too hard, that's all. A couple of days of rest and you'll feel one hundred percent better."

"Hey!" Ramona cried, pointing at Ashley's computer. "What's that?"

As Kiki turned to stare, the green letters on the computer's screen slowly transformed into a blob of shimmering, multicolored light. And once the blob had filled the whole screen, it kept growing—right into the room itself! The colors melted into each other, and Kiki could make out vague, ghostly images, images that seemed to come from . . . another world!

"What the—?" Kiki muttered, her whole body tingling with goose bumps.

"It's a hologram," Ashley explained. "Like a three-dimensional slide show."

Kiki just stared, unable to take her eyes off the expanding green blob. It was swirling and flashing now, as if it were about to explode. Then, slowly, a shape appeared inside the bizarre hologram—a shape that looked decidedly human.

44

As Kiki watched, it became clearer, like an instant photograph coming into focus.

All at once, the hologram faded, and a flesh-and-blood human being appeared where there had been only emptiness a moment before.

"Holy-moly!" gasped Ramona, leaping up from her chair. "It's Lou!"

Kiki blinked a few times to make sure her eyes weren't playing tricks on her. But no, it was definitely Lou, although she certainly didn't look the way Kiki was used to seeing her. Instead of her usual sixties-style clothing, Lou was wearing a plain ankle-length dress with a white apron tied over it. On her feet were a pair of square-heeled leather shoes with buckles, and her head was covered by a funny round cloth cap. Somehow the outfit looked very familiar to Kiki, but where had she seen it before? Then she realized—the pictures of Betsy Ross and Martha Washington that she'd seen in her history book last year when the class was studying the American Revolution.

Lou finished materializing, then looked around at Kiki, Ramona, and Charmaine with a mischievous smile. "So now you know the truth about Ashley's time-travel computer! What do you think? Merlin's a pretty outrageous little machine, isn't he?" She walked over to the computer and patted it gently on the top of its metal casing.

"Wait a minute!" Kiki said uncertainly. "Just exactly *what* is going on here?"

Lou's grin widened. "Well, I just got back from a tea party." She pulled off her cap and sat on the edge of Ashley's desk. "The *Boston* Tea Party!"

45

"I—I can't believe it," Kiki muttered.

"It's true," Ashley said. "Lou was just in the past. Seventeen seventy-three, to be exact."

Kiki felt numb all over. "Seventeen seventy-three?" she said blankly. "But . . . that's impossible!"

"Not anymore," Ashley replied. "You see, a couple of months ago I was fooling around with Merlin, working on an idea I had. I figured if I could program the computer to a 4.6897758 fractyl—that's a fraction of the fourth dimension—I'd be able—in theory, of course—to log onto different points in time."

Kiki frowned, her head reeling at the thought that Ashley just might be telling the truth. A time machine! And right here in boring old Westdale. The idea was outrageous—and Ashley's heavy-duty science talk wasn't making it any easier to understand. "A fractyl? The fourth dimension?" she said. "Come on, Ashley, you know I'm not a computer-whiz like you."

"Yeah," agreed Ramona. "What does all that mean in plain English?"

"Just be quiet and listen," Ashley said. "It's not as complicated as it sounds. A fractyl is like a fraction—a small piece of something. So I used my fractyl program to separate off a piece of the fourth dimension—that's time! Then I connected up this really neat experimental laser gun my father's company just invented. That allowed Merlin to make holograms—the three-dimensional pictures from the past that you've already seen. And finally, I connected Merlin up with the

46

research computer at the public library by using Merlin's modem. That gave him a lot more information for locating any special time. And presto! Merlin became a time machine! And I became a time-traveler!''

Kiki and Ramona gasped.

"I always knew it was possible!" Charmaine cried excitedly.

"The most amazing thing was, it actually worked!" Ashley announced triumphantly. "A few months ago, I created my first hologram of the past, and then I walked into it—right into Georgia in eighteen sixty-one! And I saw the plantation that used to belong to my mother's family, and I met my great-great-grandmother—''

"Oh, wow!" cried Charmaine. "That's fantastic! And just imagine, I thought the best way to contact the dead was through my Ouija board!" She laughed with delight. "Ashley, you're amazing!"

But Kiki just couldn't accept the idea the way Charmaine did. Her thoughts were spinning. Could it really be? she wondered. I mean, one minute Lou wasn't here, and the next moment she appeared out of nowhere. I saw that for myself—that is, unless I'm having delusions, too. Kiki glanced over at Ramona, who looked almost as flabbergasted as Kiki felt. The only one who seemed to be taking the whole thing calmly was Charmaine. But then, she'd *always* believed in impossible things. Charmaine munched on a handful of potato chips and asked eagerly, "What was it like, Lou?"

"Believe it or not, it wasn't all that different from Woodstock. There were quite a few long-haired revolutionaries grumbling about the government back in seventeen seventy-three, too!"

"Woodstock?" repeated Ramona. "You mean you went back to the huge concert in the sixties, too?"

"You bet," nodded Lou. "I even met my mother when she was a teenager. Those were two of the wildest days of my life!"

"But wait a minute," Kiki spoke up. "If you actually went back in time for a couple of days, how come no one noticed you were missing?"

"Yeah," said Ramona, "that's right. How could you have been at the Boston Tea Party? I saw you in school just a few hours ago."

"There's a glitch in the program," Ashley explained. "When I first created it, my math was slightly off. A crack in time was created, so the time-traveler just slips into that crack. As it turned out, two days in the past equals only two minutes in the present. Even though Lou lived through two days during the Revolutionary War, she missed only two minutes of our time."

"And it works the other way, too," added Lou. "Once you come back to the present, you can't return to the past for another forty-eight hours. But to the people back then, you would have only been gone two minutes."

"And . . ." Kiki began, still not quite willing to believe it, "and it really works?"

"Boy," Ashley laughed, "this afternoon you said friends shouldn't have any secrets from each

48

other. So I told you my secret—and now you refuse to believe me!"

"*I* believe you," Charmaine piped up.

"Thanks, Char," Ashley said with a smile. She turned to Kiki and Ramona. "Look, do you really think I could make up something as crazy as this? The truth is, I'm just as flipped out by this whole thing as you are. But it's true. Lou, Tina, and I have all gone back into the past. And if you want to, you can do it, too."

Kiki's heart felt like it was somersaulting inside her chest. Could it really be true? Ashley was right about one thing—the story was too incredible to be made up. Kiki peeked at Lou out of the corner of her eye, almost afraid she'd vanish as mysteriously as she'd appeared. Her Martha Washington dress, her amazing materialization out of thin air—any other explanation for those things would be just as crazy as Ashley's time-travel theory . . .

But something else Ashley had just said was echoing in Kiki's mind, also. *I can do it, too*, Kiki thought, her pulse racing out of control. Ashley was offering her the trip of her life—a time-trip. She could go anywhere in the world and anywhere in history! The possibilities were endless, and every one of them was absolutely fantastic!

Kiki grinned at Ashley and Lou. "Boy, this time-travel thing must really help when it comes to writing history essays!" Then she turned toward Ashley's computer. "Merlin, my friend, I think you're the answer to all my wildest dreams!"

Chapter Five

"NOW THAT YOU'VE ALL SWORN TO KEEP Merlin's powers a secret," Lou said, kicking off her old-fashioned shoes, "which one of you is going to try time-travel first?"

"Are you serious?" Charmaine asked excitedly.

"As long as no one finds out," Ashley said, "you're welcome to try it. But make sure you think it over first. Once I punch in the computer program and you hit the 'execute' button, there's no turning back."

"And believe me," Lou exclaimed, "traveling through time can be pretty mind-blowing. When I went back to the sixties, I found out they weren't what I'd thought they'd be. And my parents—they were completely different than I'd imagined. The whole thing was incredibly heavy."

Kiki laughed along with her friends, but deep down a little voice was saying, Well, why not do it? Life in the present sure isn't anything to throw a party about. Face it, Kiki told herself miserably, your life in the present is a total mess.

First, there were Kiki's problems with Steve. Were they really going to split up? She loved him, she needed him . . . and yet she wasn't sure she wanted to go out with him. And then there were her parents. If she told them she didn't want to go to college it would break their hearts. But if she didn't speak up soon, she'd have to put her acting career on hold for four long years.

Oh, brother, Kiki thought unhappily, I'd give anything to get out of here, away from Westdale and my parents and Steve.

But would things be any better in the past? Well, thought Kiki, there's only one way to find out . . .

"I volunteer to be the first of us to test out Ashley's crazy computer program," she announced to Ramona and Charmaine.

"Hey, hold on," Charmaine interrupted. "I'm dying to check out about a million different places in the past. You know, I could meet the most amazing wizards in history!"

"Count me in too, guys," Ramona said. She sighed. "I'd do anything to have an adventure like the ones Ashley and Lou have had."

Kiki nodded in agreement, toying with a lock of dark hair. But what adventure would she choose if she had the chance? She considered her options. She could go to Greece, where great theater was born! Elizabethan England, when Shakespeare was alive and writing the most wonderful plays ever! To the 1930s, when Hollywood was in its heyday! She thought

51

about her wish at the wishing well, her name in lights. Yes, Hollywood in the 1930s. That was the ticket. The age when they were making all those wonderful musicals and romantic comedies. It would be heaven just to get a glimpse of Fred Astaire and Ginger Rogers dancing together or Judy Garland on the set of Kiki's favorite movie ever, *The Wizard of Oz.*

Kiki let out a wistful sigh. Back in those days, she thought, a star was really a star. Glamour and glitter were the name of the game.

But could she really do it? The whole idea was so crazy! Even now she could hardly believe it wasn't some sort of incredible joke.

"So," Ashley asked, "who's going to be first?"

"Me!" three voices called out at the same time.

"Well, you can't all go at once," Ashley said. "How about if you draw straws?" She opened the top drawer of her desk and took out three different-length pencils, wrapping a scarf around them so that only the points showed.

Ramona chose first, her hand trembling just a bit as she slid one of the pencils out of the scarf. It was a worn stump. "Oh, no," she moaned, "an obvious loser."

Charmaine didn't do much better.

"Yippee!" Kiki whooped, plucking a shiny, new pencil out of Ashley's hand. She could barely believe it. She'd won! "Hollywood, here I come!" she cried excitedly.

She licked her lips, ready to tell Ashley to set

Merlin up to send her back in time . . . but the words didn't come out. Suddenly a tiny tingle of panic shot through Kiki's stomach. A moment ago, escaping into the past had seemed like a great idea. Now that she was faced with the reality, Kiki was beginning to feel terrified. "Are you sure it takes only two minutes, Ashley?"

Ashley nodded. "It's pretty confusing at first. So much happens to you in the past that you just can't believe it's only two minutes in the present. Plus, it's not always the way you expect it to be in the past."

"And when you come back to the present, you feel completely confused," Lou added. "Tonight was my third time-trip, so I'm starting to get the hang of it. But to tell you the truth, I still feel pretty dazed." She took a pair of jeans and a yellow paisley shirt from the end of Ashley's bed. "Maybe if I get out of this eighteenth-century dress and put my real clothes on . . ."

Kiki was feeling more stunned by the second. Here she was, sitting around with her friends, calmly discussing time-travel as if it were the most natural thing in the world. And to make the whole thing even more unbelievable, she was actually about to go back to the past herself.

What am I getting myself into? she wondered nervously. Some weird adventure in a time when I haven't even been born yet. I'll be totally out of place. Everyone will be wearing old-fashioned clothes. The newest movies will be old films I've seen on late-night television. People won't know a thing about what's happened in the past fifty years . . .

She glanced at Ashley and Lou. They'd both gone back in time and neither of them looked any worse for it. In fact, they seemed absolutely thrilled. Besides, Kiki asked herself, what could possibly go wrong?

Immediately, a dozen horrible possibilities popped into her mind. What if I got stuck in the past? Or died while I was there before I'd actually been born. Is that possible? With a shudder, Kiki pushed all the doubts from her mind. Nothing terrible had happened to Ashley and the others, and there was no reason to think anything terrible would happen to her. Besides, she couldn't pass up a chance to see the old-time Hollywood she'd imagined countless times—to see it with her own eyes!

"Speaking of clothes," Lou said, zipping herself into her jeans, "Kiki, you're going to need some thirties-style clothes. I mean, you'd look pretty out of place in *that* outfit."

Kiki looked down at her red jeans and gray suede boots. She laughed. With her baggy black-and-white-checked blouse, it wasn't exactly the kind of outfit you'd expect to see Bette Davis or Carole Lombard wearing!

"You'll just have to wing it," Lou said. "That's what I did. When I left for my trip to the Boston Tea Party, I was wearing an old-fashioned flannel nightgown that I hadn't put on since my mother bought it for me last year." She giggled. "I told everybody my clothes were funny because I'd been living among the Cherokee Indians for the last five years. Then I borrowed a dress from a chambermaid who worked in the Bird-in-hand Tavern."

"Well, okay . . ." Kiki said uncertainly.

Ashley motioned Ramona away from Merlin and sat down in front of the computer. Carefully, she punched in a series of commands. "Well, Kiki, what year do you want to go back to, and where exactly do you want to be?"

Kiki thought quickly. "Well, my favorite movie is *The Wizard of Oz* . . ."

"When did that come out?"

"Nineteen thirty-nine," Kiki answered. "It was one of MGM's biggest hits."

"Okay, how's this?" Ashley asked, tapping out a few words on Merlin's keyboard. "MGM Studios . . . Hollywood, California . . . nineteen thirty-nine."

Kiki nodded slowly, still trying to figure out if she really wanted to go through with this crazy adventure. Ramona came over and threw her arms around Kiki in an excited hug. "Have a fantastic time," she said.

"Yeah," Lou chimed in. "It's going to be a blast. But remember to watch what you say. If you blurt out something about NASA or rock 'n' roll or mopeds or other modern-day stuff, everyone will think you're nuts."

"Oh, right," Kiki said. It was so strange to hear her friends casually wishing her a good trip, knowing she'd be half a century away in a matter of minutes.

"Okay," Ashley said. "All you have to do, Kiki, is hit the 'execute' key. Then you're on your way to the thirties!"

Kiki gulped. She'd daydreamed about this moment for years, and now that it was actually here, she was on the verge of backing out. I've *got* to go through with it, she ordered herself. Steeling her nerves, she marched purposefully over to Merlin. Before she could think it over another time, she pushed the button.

For an instant, nothing happened. Good, I knew it was all some silly joke, Kiki thought, the chicken in her suddenly getting the best of her. But then the blob appeared, pulsating on Merlin's screen and growing. The swirl of colors expanded into the room, engulfing Kiki in a rainbow cloud.

"Relax," she heard Ashley say. "You're going to have the time of your life."

But Kiki couldn't relax. Suddenly she felt very frightened. This was no daydream. It was *real!* Her heart pounded as she watched her hand, still resting on Merlin's keypad, beginning to fade. Her body tingled all over and she felt herself being sucked down the long corridor of time.

"Wait!" she cried fearfully. But her words only echoed hollowly somewhere in between the decades of time. Oh, Steve, she thought. Mom, Dad. Will I ever see you again?

Kiki felt like Dorothy being swept into the Land of Oz by the tornado. Judy Garland's famous line from the movie popped into her mind—"Toto, I have a feeling we're not in Kansas anymore." Or Westdale, Connecticut, either, Kiki thought.

Then all at once the whirling stopped, and the tingling in her hands and feet faded slowly. She blinked a few times. The scene before her was strange—but very familiar, too.

She was standing next to a small, round, cardboard house with a yellow roof. Dozens of colorfully dressed midgets danced around a spiral-shaped yellow cardboard road singing "Ding dong, the witch is dead!"

"Now I *know* I'm not in Westdale," Kiki gasped. She'd seen this place a dozen times before . . . on TV airings of *The Wizard of Oz!* But then it had been only a two-dimensional picture. Now, it was a living, breathing, singing, dancing reality!

Chapter Six

"CUT!" A DEEP VOICE SHOUTED. ABRUPTLY, the music ended and the midgets stopped dancing. "Hey, you! The tall one in back! What are you doing on the set? This is the Munchkin scene!"

With a start, Kiki realized that the voice was yelling at *her*. The movie cameras had stopped rolling, and everyone was staring at her with obvious irritation.

"Thanks a bunch," one of the midgets muttered under his breath. "Now we'll have to do the whole stupid dance over again."

Kiki didn't know which way to turn. Her cheeks burned with embarrassment, and the blazing movie lights made her feel even more obvious and out of place. "How do I get out of here?" she squeaked in panic.

"Follow the yellow brick road," a tough-looking Munchkin wisecracked.

Kiki turned, searching for some way off the set. A pretty young woman in a blue-and-white-checked dress began walking toward her. Holy Hollywood, Kiki thought with astonishment.

That's Judy Garland! She couldn't be coming over to talk to *me.* Kiki stared, unable to move a muscle, as her all-time favorite movie star approached her.

Garland stopped in front of Kiki and smiled warmly. "It's just that everybody's in a bad mood because it's past dinnertime and the director wants to do one more take."

Kiki knew she should say something, but her voice seemed to have gone on strike. Here I am, she thought, standing face-to-face with Judy Garland! How amazing! She's a star—a show biz legend!

While Kiki stood there gaping, Judy reached down to scoop up the little dog that was yapping at her heels. "Meet Toto," she said with a giggle. She held out one of the dog's paws, and Kiki, finally managing a smile, shook it gently. "Hi, Toto," she said.

"Listen, young lady, would you mind telling me exactly what you're doing on my set?" an angry voice broke in.

Kiki turned to see the director storming across the set toward her. All at once, Kiki had the terrible urge to giggle. What could she possibly say to the raging director? "Don't mind me, I won't even be born for about another thirty years, so I can't really be standing here ruining your movie." Or, "A sixteen-year-old genius friend of mine back in Westdale, Connecticut, has just invented a way to make dreams come alive with her souped-up computer." It was all true, but if she said any of it out loud, the entire

59

movie crew would think she was out of her gourd!

Kiki bit her lip, the hot lights beating down on her relentlessly. If she couldn't tell the truth, what *should* she say? Her mind went blank and she just stared down at the yellow cardboard road and Judy Garland's shiny red patent-leather shoes—the ruby slippers of *The Wizard of Oz* fame, she realized with a start.

"Hey," the director barked rudely, "I asked you a question, and I want an answer. Now!"

"Aww, knock it off, Vic," came a sassy female voice. A young woman with tightly permed, bleached-blond hair dashed across the set and stepped in between Kiki and the director. "Can't you see you're scaring the poor kid?" she reprimanded. She turned to Kiki with a crooked smile and a jaunty I-know-how-to-handle-these-types wink. "I'm Doris," she said. "What's your name?"

"K-Kiki," she managed to stammer. "Kiki Wykowski."

Doris looked Kiki up and down. "Dressed in *that* weird outfit, I'd guess you're working on that serial they're shooting next door. What's it called—*Flash Gordon*, or something like that?"

Kiki gazed down at her red jeans. Doris didn't know it, but she had just given Kiki a compliment. The evil aliens in the old science fiction series she'd seen on cable TV always wore the greatest outfits. Kiki shuffled her feet, holding back a giggle, and muttered, "Well, uh—"

"You just wandered onto the wrong set, is that it?" Doris prompted with a kind smile.

"Um . . . yes," Kiki nodded, grateful for an excuse. "Yes, I guess I did."

"Okay, come on, kid." Doris grabbed Kiki's arm and led her away from Judy Garland and the director. As they walked off the set, Kiki glanced back over her shoulder. The director was staring after her with his hands on his hips and a sour expression on his face. Judy Garland was kneeling down, petting Toto. Kiki's eyes met the star's, and Judy smiled and waved.

She waved to me, Kiki thought with awe. Judy Garland actually waved to me! Kiki decided right there that even if the rest of her adventure was the pits, it would all be worth it just to have had Judy Garland smile and say a few words to her. Of course, she would have given anything to be allowed to stay for just fifteen minutes and watch the star perform. That would really be a dream come alive. But the director's grimace was enough to show Kiki that it wouldn't be a very good idea to ask if she could stick around.

Doris led Kiki off the soundstage where *The Wizard of Oz* was being shot. "Good luck, kid," she said, opening a door marked "Exit" and giving Kiki an encouraging little shove.

As Kiki stepped outside, the heavy door slammed shut behind her. For a moment, she just stood there wondering what in the world she should do next. Things are happening too fast, she thought. One second I'm sitting in

61

Ashley's bedroom eating potato chips, and the next second I'm in the middle of a 1939 movie set, meeting Judy Garland in the flesh! And now I'm— Kiki looked around, realizing she didn't have any idea where Doris had dumped her.

She was standing on a wide, dirt street lined with soundstages—the huge barnlike structures where movie sets were created and pictures filmed. Elaborately costumed actresses and actors hurried about their business, kicking up dust from the dirt street as they rushed in and out of the buildings.

Kiki was thrilled to realize that each one of these buildings meant one more movie was being shot—why, there were dozens of them! If only I could wander through them all, Kiki daydreamed, watching the great MGM films of 1939 come to life! She shook her head, giggling. But imagine getting kicked off each set the way I got kicked off *The Wizard of Oz* set. I'm sure everyone wouldn't be quite as nice as that woman Doris was.

A man in loose, pleated pants, a vest and jacket, and a bow tie pushed past Kiki. "Hey, you're blocking the road," he said, annoyed.

Kiki watched the man hurry away. Great costume, she thought. He must be in a movie set in the past. Suddenly Kiki caught her breath. That was no costume. The man was wearing normal street clothes—the kind that were popular in the late 1930s! She glanced down the street again, amazed to realize that all those women who seemed so wonderfully old-fashioned in their frilly dresses and great-looking hats were actually in the height of style.

Wow, they sure look fabulous, Kiki thought. She tried to picture all her friends dressed in outfits like these, and Steve in a 1930s' suit with a bow tie. She sighed. Sometimes she felt like the modern-day kids really missed out when it came to glamour and style.

There were a lot of costumed people too, rushing in and out of soundstages or waiting for their scenes to be shot. Kiki couldn't believe how busy MGM was, even though it was way past dinnertime, as Judy Garland had told her. But movie studios were notorious for their long hours. A few men in Civil War costumes lounged around with a cowboy and an Indian with an ax sticking out of his head. A group of women in Egyptian slave outfits stood drinking coffee together.

Kiki watched a man walking quickly toward her. As he got close, she could see a puffy black eye and dried blood caked all over his neck and face. Kiki let out a gasp and jumped back in disgust.

A few people turned and stared at her as if she were crazy, but the man just laughed. "Great makeup job, huh?" he asked with a grin. "Tim Weird does excellent work. If you're ever in a death scene, ask for him. He's the best on the lot."

Kiki nodded weakly. Her heart was still pounding from the shock. I should have realized it was only makeup, she told herself. Still, it looked so real!

Feeling a little dazed, Kiki turned in the opposite direction and wandered up the street, staring wide-eyed at the spectacle around her. She passed a group of Roman warriors carrying swords and shields. A woman wearing a gorilla suit and carrying the head in her arms strolled along with a soldier carrying a machine gun. Kiki smiled and the woman winked. Kiki giggled to herself. Once she accepted that MGM Studios was really a big, crazy zoo, it was kind of fun to watch this wild street show. And who knew what wonderful, famous stars were working behind the closed doors of the sound studios!

Kiki stopped to watch a group of men carrying large scenery-flats painted with the New York skyline. She recognized the Empire State Building, but the Twin Towers were missing, along with three-quarters of the skyscrapers Kiki knew were part of modern-day New York. A trio of women in flowing evening gowns walked by, chatting with a man in a Count Dracula costume.

Slowly, the truth was sinking in. I'm really here, Kiki thought with delight. Hollywood, 1939! Walking along with her head held high, she could almost pretend that she was on her way to shoot a scene in a soon-to-be-famous film. Maybe a love scene with Gary Cooper, or Jimmy Stewart, or . . .

Clark Gable! Kiki's heart leapt into her throat.

That handsome man with the mustache who'd just walked past her—could it really be the star? She turned and hurried after him, but before she could get a good look, he disappeared into one of the buildings. Oh, well, Kiki whispered happily, Clark Gable's back is better than no Clark Gable at all.

A woman in an outlandish feathered outfit hurried toward Kiki. "Strange outfit you've got on, honey," the woman said as she passed by.

Kiki stared after her in amazement, watching her peacock-feathered headdress bob back and forth. "How can she say *my* outfit's strange when she's wearing *that* getup?" Kiki asked out loud. But she realized that her regular old 1980s' clothes were really out of place in 1939, even in a movie studio. She shuddered to think of how she would have seemed if she'd asked Merlin to drop her *outside* the MGM building. And I'm not even one of the kids in Westdale who dresses weird, Kiki thought.

Okay, Kiki decided, my next project is to find some normal clothes—at least normal for 1939— unless I want to spend two days pretending I'm an actress in a science fiction movie. Suddenly, the crazy truth of her situation hit her. "Gosh," she breathed, "I'm going to be here for forty-eight hours." Two whole days in Hollywood, 1939!

But according to Ashley, two days in the past equaled only two minutes in the present. That meant that back in Westdale, her friends were still sitting around Ashley's room, awaiting her return. At home, Mama and Papa would be closing the store and starting dinner. And Steve—what was he doing? Did he miss her? Or was he glad they'd decided to put their relationship on hold? Back in the present, only about half an hour had passed since they'd had that horrible conversation. Did Steve wish they could erase those few minutes the way she did?

Kiki realized with a pang that she *did* miss Steve. Even in the midst of this incredible adventure, she missed steady, predictable old Steve. Why? She couldn't figure it out. Being in Hollywood was the only thing she ever really wanted. But now that she was here, she felt just the tiniest bit homesick, especially for Steve.

Kiki pushed the subtle little feeling to the back of her mind. She was here now, and it was wonderful, and that was all she needed to think about—other than finding herself some more appropriate clothing.

The sun was already beginning to set and a cool evening breeze wafted across Kiki's shoulders. The palm trees peeking out above the tops of the buildings swayed gently in the breeze. California! She'd gotten so excited about actually being at MGM that she'd forgotten all about being on the sunny West Coast. She stared into the cloudless pinkish purple sky. Beaches, kidney-shaped swimming pools, sunsets! This was going to be one great vacation from freezing cold, slush-covered Westdale.

"Coming through! Coming through!"

Kiki jumped out of the way just seconds before someone whizzed by pushing a large rack of costumes and clothing. "Hey," she called out, ready to tell the guy off for not looking where he was going. "Excuse me!" she shouted, running after the rack of costumes. "Where are you taking those clothes?"

"To Wardrobe," the man replied. "It's time to close up the set. Why?"

"I'll take them over there," she said in what she hoped was a commanding tone of voice. "The director wants you back on the set right now."

"Oh, okay. Thanks." The man pushed the rack of clothes toward Kiki and started back the way he'd come.

It worked! Kiki thought with delight. It actually worked! Grinning triumphantly, she grabbed hold of the rack and hurried up the street. Now, she thought, if I can just find someplace to change.

Chapter Seven

KIKI STEPPED OUT FROM BEHIND THE TWO-
story building marked "WARDROBE," wobbling
uncertainly in a pair of brown high heels that
were much too big for her. Her new dress was
a green-and-white-flowered print with padded
shoulders, a tight waist, and a flowing, calf-
length skirt. It wasn't exactly glamorous, but at
least now she didn't look like an alien from a
science fiction thriller, lost in a world that wasn't
her own—though that description certainly fit
Kiki better than her high heels. She took a few
more unsteady steps, tucking her folded Westdale clothes inconspicuously under her arm.

Kiki had left the rack of costumes near the back
door of the building. Well, I said I'd take the
clothes to Wardrobe, she told herself. I just didn't
mention I'd be borrowing a few things first!

But when Kiki turned, she found a burly man
in a security-guard uniform gazing at her curiously. Uh-oh, here comes trouble, she thought
as the guard began walking toward her.

"Are you one of the extras from *Stars in Her
Eyes?*" he asked.

"Um, er—" Kiki began, wondering if it was better to say yes or no.

"Well, Mr. Lester said to tell everyone that shooting's finished for the day. You better go in and get your stuff," he added, pointing across the street to one of the soundstages. "I'm clocking off over here in half an hour."

"Oh, okay. Thanks." Kiki took a couple of wobbly steps toward the building and glanced back over her shoulder. The guard was still watching her. If I don't go in, she thought, he'll figure out I don't belong here and throw me out. There was only one thing to do. With what she hoped was a confident smile, she turned and walked through the soundstage door.

Once inside, Kiki found herself standing on another set, but this one was a little less strange than the Munchkin scene in *The Wizard of Oz*. The room had been decorated as an old-fashioned living room—not old-fashioned, Kiki corrected herself, *if* you were from 1939. A few overstuffed chairs were placed around a marble coffee table. Lace curtains hid the cardboard backdrop. A gramophone with a windup crank—the kind Kiki had seen in countless old movies—stood on one side.

But the stage was empty of people. Where is everybody? Kiki wondered, taking in the unmanned cameras and the empty director's chair. Well, she decided, the guard said it was quitting time. I guess everyone's gone home. She was just about to walk over for a closer look at the set when a platinum blond in a tight-fitting suit with a fur collar came striding onto the stage. A middle-aged man with thinning dark hair followed angrily on her heels. Quickly, Kiki ducked into the shadows.

"You can't just walk off the picture like this!" the man was shouting. "You're under contract!"

Wincing dramatically, the blond placed her hand in the small of her back and said, "My back is killing me, Marty. My contract says nothin' about me workin' when I'm sick."

"Sick!" Marty yelled "*I'm* the one who's sick, Collette—sick and tired of all your excuses. The last time we worked together I had to hold up the picture a whole week while you flew off to Mexico to divorce husband number three. Now it's number four, right? And I suppose you've got number five all lined up to take his place."

Collette's eyes narrowed to emerald slits. "Well, one thing's for sure, Marty," she sneered, "it ain't gonna be you!" With that, she flounced off the set, heading straight for the spot where Kiki was hiding.

"Hey," Marty yelled after her, "you can't leave! Who am I going to get to star in my picture?"

But Collette kept walking. Until she spotted Kiki. For a brief second she paused and stared at her as if she'd just come upon a disgusting little bug. Then she turned to Marty and yelled, "You need someone to take my place?" She grabbed Kiki and pulled her into the light. "For all I care, you can make *Stars in Her Eyes* with

70

her.'' She let out a peal of shrill laughter and strolled out the door.

Kiki stood there, feeling embarrassed and scared, while Marty glared at her. Would he have her thrown out of MGM? Arrested for trespassing? She started backing toward the door. "Um, gee, I'm sorry," she stammered. "I—I was just leaving . . .''

But Marty's expression had softened. "You know," he muttered, gazing at her thoughtfully, "it would serve Collette right." He put his hands on his hips and smiled smugly. "Young lady," he asked, "how would you like to be a movie star?''

Kiki stared at Marty in disbelief. Then, all at once, she was absolutely sure she was going to faint. Those words—she'd dreamed a million times that someone would say them to her. But . . . it couldn't be true. This Marty guy, whoever he was, had to be joking. Either that or her ears were playing tricks on her. "Uh, could you repeat that?'' she asked, positive she hadn't heard the man right. "Are you serious?''

Marty shook his head. "Never mind," he replied. "It was just a crazy idea. It would never work. You probably don't know the first thing about acting.''

"Oh, yes I do!'' Kiki cried indignantly. Joke or no joke, she wasn't going to let anyone tell her she couldn't act. "I've played Maria in *West S*—'' Suddenly she broke off. *West Side Story* hadn't been written until the 1950s. Marty wouldn't know about it for another twenty years!

Marty looked skeptical. "*West?* Never heard of it. So you say you're an actress, huh? I had you figured for a script girl or a wardrobe assistant." He looked Kiki up and down. "What are you doing here? You're not on the crew of *Stars in Her Eyes.*"

"Uh, no," Kiki said, thinking fast. "I . . . just finished working on . . . on *The Wizard of Oz.*"

"Oh, yeah?" Marty said, looking interested. "What's your role?"

"It's just a bit part," Kiki replied, feeling more courageous with every passing second. She wasn't really lying, she decided, just acting out a part—the part of a future star trying to talk her way into her first big break. "But then I just arrived in Hollywood," she continued. "Before that I was acting in plays back east." Well, she thought, at least *that* part's true.

Marty moved closer. "Hmm," he murmured, gazing at Kiki like a buyer at a horse auction. "The hair's all wrong . . . and the makeup . . . but that can be fixed."

"Excuse me," Kiki said, squirming under his gaze. "Are you the director of this picture?"

"That's right. Marty Lester's the name." He smiled an oily smile. "What did you say yours was?"

"Kiki Wykowski."

Marty grimaced and shook his head. "Wrong!"

"But that really is my name," she protested.

"And it's about as exciting as Frances Gumm."

"What?" Kiki asked with a puzzled expression.

"Frances Gumm. That's Judy Garland's real name. But can you imagine *The Wizard of Oz*, starring Frances Gumm? No, of course not," he continued, not waiting for Kiki to answer. "The public expects movie stars to have sexy, sophisticated names, so that's what they get." He studied Kiki. "If you're right for the part, we'll have to do something about that. But first things first. Let's do an audition."

In an instant, Kiki felt her stomach filling with butterflies. No, not butterflies—a whole flock of wild birds! Back home, auditions had never upset her. But then, back home the only roles she'd ever tried out for were in high-school plays. This was the big time—a real Hollywood movie. If she landed the part, she'd be on the road to stardom! But . . . stardom in the wrong time.

Wait, Kiki felt like crying, this is all mixed up. My *parents* aren't even alive yet. I've got less than two days left here. We'll *never* be able to shoot this film in *that* amount of time. Why couldn't this have happened to me in the '80s, where I would really be able to follow through with it? Why can't Mr. Lester come back home with me and make the movie there?

But Kiki knew she couldn't say any of those things. Sighing, she felt the glittering prize of stardom slipping out of her reach.

"Grab that script on top of the gramophone," said Marty Lester, unaware of Kiki's inner turmoil. "Stand over there by the sofa." He sank easily into the director's chair, still scrutinizing Kiki. "You've got a good face," he said, "kind of sweet and innocent, which is what we're looking for in this film."

"But Collette wasn't—"

"Sweet and innocent?" Marty laughed loudly. "Far from it. But she got her start that way, and now she's trying to hold on to the image. So far, her fans still buy it—but not for long, if you ask me." He flashed Kiki another one of his oily smiles. "Okay, let's hear you read the speech on the top of page six."

With trembling hands, Kiki opened the script to the right section. Oh, well, Kiki shrugged. I might as well give this audition a shot, even though I'm fifty years too young to accept the part. It'll make a great story, though, to tell Ashley and Ramona and everyone when I get back to Westdale.

She quickly glanced over the words. The speech was all about how she was going to leave her small, midwestern town and her sickly mother to make it big in Hollywood. Her last lines were, "But I'll make good, Ma. I swear it. And then I'll send you the money you need to have your operation. Ma? Ma! Don't die on me now, Ma." Then she was supposed to burst into tears.

Oh, no, Kiki thought, this is so corny! But then she remembered how she'd felt watching

Flashdance just a few days ago with Steve—on an evening that wasn't going to happen for another fifty years, she reminded herself.

Flashdance was every bit as corny as the script she was about to read for Marty Lester, wasn't it? But that hadn't mattered to Kiki. Jennifer Beals's performance had been completely engrossing, despite a couple of very silly lines.

"Okay, let's get started," Marty ordered.

Kiki took a deep breath and closed her eyes, concentrating on the words and trying to get into the right mood. The birds in her stomach were still flapping madly, but she forced herself to ignore them. Opening her eyes, she looked straight into Marty Lester's face and began, "Ma, you gotta understand, I got show business in my blood . . ."

Slowly, Kiki felt the familiar magic beginning, the magic that made her love acting so completely. She was falling deep into the part, becoming one with the character, living out a secret side of her own personality. And why not? It certainly wasn't a hard role. Especially not for Kiki, who could imagine herself saying the same kinds of things—though not in quite such a corny way—to her own mother over a plate of sliced roast beef back at Nick's Deli. Soon there was nothing left in the world for Kiki except that part—no time-travel, no problems at home, not even any Marty Lester.

For the next few minutes, Kiki *was* that young girl saying good-bye to her ailing mother. She was practically sobbing when she got to the last line. "Ma! Don't die on me now, Ma," she cried. And then she let loose a flood of tears and dramatic sniffles.

At last, Kiki wiped away the tears with the back of her hand and dared to focus back on the director. Marty Lester sat imposingly in his chair, his face as blank as an empty chalkboard. Kiki's heart sank to a miserable low. He hated me. With a sigh, she turned and started to walk off the set.

"Hey, hang on, kid," Marty called. "Where ya goin'?"

"Well, I—"

"You did all right." Marty broke into a toothy grin. "We'll have to give you a screen test tomorrow morning, just to make sure you're photogenic. But I really think you can pull it off." He chuckled. "And wouldn't that put Collette's snooty nose out of joint? A talented young nobody like you filling her spot. You know, I think that with a little help, you could become a bigger star than Collette, too." He walked over and patted Kiki on the arm. "Tomorrow's screen test is just a formality. You're on this picture—and if you do all right, we'll put you on a couple more. You leave everything to me and there'll be big things in store for you at MGM."

Kiki felt like jumping for joy. I've only been in Hollywood for a couple of hours, she thought with amazement, and already I have the lead in a feature film! It's just the way I always dreamed it would be—only this time it's for real! Or was it? Could she really accept the part, knowing she was going to disappear like a puff of smoke after the second day of filming?

Kiki knew what Steve would say—don't start anything you won't be able to finish. People will be counting on you, and then you'll let them all down. Besides, what good will it do you to shoot only two days of a film? No one will ever get to see your performance. Better to wait for another offer to come along. One you can really accept. Sure, that's what practical, logical Steve would say.

But Kiki didn't *want* to be practical. She was being given the role of a lifetime—not the character in the movie, but the one she'd be playing off the screen. For two days she could be a big-time Hollywood movie star, just like she'd always dreamed—fancy dinners, silk gowns, outrageous parties—she'd be nuts to pass up the chance.

Deep down, Kiki knew Steve's way was right. But it was exactly Steve's calm logic that was driving Kiki crazy about him lately. If she'd missed him earlier in the evening, suddenly she was thrilled to be three thousand miles and half a century away from him. Far enough to do the impractical, illogical thing, just this once.

Kiki had to admit to herself that she'd never had any intention of turning down the job, not even for an instant. This was truly an offer she couldn't refuse. And besides, if the filming went well, she might even be able to convince Ashley to send her back again to finish shooting it.

Kiki glanced over at Marty. ''Yeah,'' he was

saying, "Collette's gonna choke on her champagne when she finds out a total unknown has picked up her part." As Kiki watched Marty's greasy smile creep onto his face, she felt a tickle of uneasiness. It's almost as if he's only using me to get back at her, Kiki thought. Maybe he doesn't really care about me or my acting after all.

Oh, well, she thought, pushing aside her doubts. Who cares? I'll be starring in a Hollywood movie. That's what *really* counts.

"Take the script with you, hon," Marty was saying. "We'll be shooting the first fifteen pages tomorrow. I want you here at six A.M. sharp with your lines memorized."

"Fifteen pages!" Kiki gasped. Back at O. Henry they were still working on page five of *The Pirates of Penzance*, and that was after a full week of rehearsal!

Marty nodded. "Thanks to Collette and her tantrums, we're already two days behind schedule on this picture. We've got to make up for lost time." He put his arm around Kiki's shoulder and led her toward the door. "Tomorrow morning we'll give you a quick screen test. Then we'll have you go up to the front office to sign a contract and meet the publicity staff. After that, we'll work on your new image." He steered her out onto the street. "Tomorrow at six," he said. "Don't be late."

Out on the dirt-covered street, Kiki saw that the lot was almost deserted now. Most of the actors were gone and the few people who walked by were all in street clothes. It was already dark, the streetlamps were on, and a cool breeze rustled the tops of the palm trees. Kiki shivered slightly.

Everything had happened so quickly that she barely knew what to think or how to feel. One part of her was incredibly happy. Just being offered the role in *Stars in Her Eyes* was a dream come true, and it proved she really did have star quality. But another part of her was hopelessly frustrated. She'd finally been given the chance to become a star—to fulfill every fantasy she'd ever had! And she was going to have to throw it all away and go back to being just plain Kiki Wykowski, a high-school girl with big dreams.

Kiki walked down the dusty street, kicking at a few stones with her wobbly high-heeled shoes. All in all, she decided, the trip had been pretty fantastic so far. But she had the sinking feeling that things were going to take a turn for the worse right about now. Staring around at the dark, deserted lot, Kiki was completely alone. She had no place to go, and she was hungry and exhausted. Back in Westdale, Ashley and the others still hadn't finished that first bag of potato chips. Her parents and sisters would be getting ready for a delicious home-cooked dinner. Even Steve's mother's notoriously bad cooking would have been a welcome meal to Kiki right now. How she longed for the comfort of her own bed to fall into. But there were only the empty, locked sets all around her.

The chilly breeze blew a little harder, cutting

through Kiki's thin dress. She sighed and sat down in the doorway of one of the soundstages. If only she could slip into her jeans and long-sleeved shirt. But looking like a science fiction freak certainly wasn't going to solve any of her problems. She'd just have to stick with the dress and freeze a little.

A woman in a blue pillbox hat hurried by. "Better get home now, dear," she said, smiling kindly at Kiki. "They're about to lock up the lot."

Kiki bit her lip. Home. She wished she could get back there. Right now, the boring life she'd so wanted to leave behind seemed pretty enticing. She'd stuff herself with her mother's incredible chicken-and-dumpling soup and top it off with her father's famous chocolate cake. Then she'd get on the phone and fix everything up with Steve. Maybe he'd even come over and watch an old movie on TV with her. What she wouldn't do to feel his warm, comforting arms around her right this minute.

But, Kiki knew, she wouldn't be able to get home for another day and a half. What was she going to do until then? If only I'd brought some money. Five dollars would go a very long way here in 1939. It was amazing to think that at home, five bucks wouldn't even cover the cost of one music cassette, while here—she thought back to some of the coffee-shop scenes she'd seen in her favorite old movies—you could get a whole meal for twenty-five cents. Five dollars would have been enough for a delicious dinner *and* a nice warm hotel room, with plenty to spare.

Kiki slipped her aching feet out of the brown high heels. But I didn't bring any money with me, she scolded herself. Not even a cent. In fact, I wasn't prepared for this trip in any way whatsoever! I jumped into this time-travel thing as if it were a trip to the girls' room at school, not a journey through the fourth dimension! I should have thought it all out! I should have at least brought along a few necessities.

So what am I going to do now? Kiki asked herself. The image of walking the streets all night or sleeping on a park bench flashed through her mind like a shot of fear. She could see herself coming in to the first day of shooting *Stars in Her Eyes* tomorrow. She'd be sleepless and dirty. "Sorry, sweetheart," she could hear Marty Lester saying, "I must have been out of my mind to hire a bum like you. But since we never signed a contract, it's no problem. You're off the picture and"—he would point angrily toward the door—"off the set!"

Kiki felt the tears welling up in her eyes. She tucked her feet underneath her and hugged her body, trying desperately to stay warm. She'd never been so scared and alone and frustrated in all her life.

"Well, well, well," a familiar voice broke into Kiki's misery. "If it isn't the Munchkin who grew too tall."

Kiki looked up to find Doris, the woman who had helped her out on the set of *The Wizard of*

81

Oz, smiling down at her broadly. Kiki slipped her feet back into her shoes and stood up quickly, feeling embarrassed.

Doris laughed, patting a few loose strands of her bottle-blond hair. "You know, you remind me of a lost cat," she said. "Give it a little milk, and it keeps coming back for more."

Kiki smiled sheepishly. "I guess I am kind of lost."

Doris took a close look at her and frowned. "What is it with you, kid? You got no place to stay?"

"No, not really," Kiki admitted, thinking fast to come up with a believable explanation. "You see, I, uh—"

"I know the feeling," Doris said. "It wasn't too long ago that I was in your shoes. Suitcase in my hand and stars in my eyes. All the way from Kansas, just like Dorothy. The only thing I gave a hoot about was a shot at the big time—a leading role in a Hollywood picture. 'Course, now that I'm here, all I can come up with is a production assistant's job." She sighed. "How 'bout you? Where do you come from?"

"Connecticut," Kiki said. But not the Connecticut anyone around here knows about, she added to herself. Why, if Doris knew where I was really from, she'd be scared to pieces.

Doris chuckled. "I got locked out of my first apartment on account of all the back rent I owed. I'll bet the same thing happened to you, huh?"

Kiki nodded, grateful that Doris had come up

with her own explanation. And it wasn't too far off, either, she thought. I did come here with stars in my eyes, all the way from Connecticut. The only difference is, I had to travel across time to get here!

"Good thing I'm a sucker for lost cats," Doris said, putting her arm around Kiki's shoulder and leading her up the street. "My apartment isn't much to look at, but it's better than nothing."

"You mean, I can stay at your place?" Kiki gasped, hardly daring to believe her ears.

"That's the general idea. Unless you got a room waiting for you at the Hollywood Plaza Hotel."

Kiki laughed, relief and gratitude flooding through her. She glanced over at Doris. Her new friend talked tough, and with her halo of peroxided hair and fire-engine-red lipstick, she didn't look like your typical fairy godmother. But that's exactly how Kiki was beginning to think of her. Her crooked smile was genuinely sweet. Kiki felt sure she'd seen that smile before, but she couldn't remember where. "Your apartment will be just super!" she said gratefully.

Doris smiled and gave Kiki a reassuring pat on the shoulder. "Come on, kid, let's go home."

Chapter Eight

KIKI SETTLED INTO THE UPHOLSTERED seat of the huge, old-fashioned black car.

"It's a hunk of junk," Doris was saying, "but it gets me where I want to go."

"Junk?" Kiki blurted out. She'd read the model name on the car's grill, and she knew a Packard, circa 1934, was no old jalopy. "This car is an antique! It's probably worth thousands of dollars!"

"Are you kidding?" Doris asked in disbelief. "It cost me a hundred and fifty bucks used, and it isn't even worth that. But if you want to get around to auditions, you've got to have a car."

"Oh, right," Kiki muttered as Doris started the engine. "I—I must be more tired than I thought," she explained lamely. "I guess I don't really know much about cars."

Ugh, Kiki berated herself, how can you be so dense? This is 1939, so Doris's dented Packard is just another secondhand car. She sighed. It really would be something else, though, to drive this car into the parking lot at O. Henry High. Back in the '80s, everyone would flip over it.

Doris steered the Packard through MGM's front gates and out onto the streets of Hollywood. Taking in the quaint buildings and two-lane streets, Kiki gasped out loud. Somewhere in the back of her mind, she'd been expecting to find a modern-day Los Angeles outside the crazy, make-believe world she was leaving, the kind of Los Angeles she'd seen in fan magazines. The kind she'd imagined driving through in a silver limo on her way to accept her first Academy Award. But, of course, that Hollywood didn't exist yet, and the one Kiki found herself in was fifty years out-of-date.

There were no glass and steel skyscrapers, no shopping centers or malls or giant supermarkets, no roller-skate rental places or video stores. Not even a McDonald's or a Burger King. The city was made up of sleepy little stores and houses with red tile roofs and a few larger buildings built out of brick. None of the stores was much bigger than Nick's Eastside Deli back home in Westdale. Kiki couldn't believe it. To her, Hollywood in 1939 looked like a small town!

Doris laughed. "It sure is a far cry from Connecticut, isn't it, kid?"

You don't know the half of it! Kiki thought as she stared curiously out the window. Newspaper boys in knickers hawked the evening papers in front of barber shops with spinning barber poles. Shoeshine boys worked for a nickel.

As the Packard cruised up Washington Boulevard, the streetlights came on. But they weren't the tall, bright, aluminum ones that lighted

Westdale's streets each night. These were dimmer, giving off a yellowish light, and the short iron poles were embellished with designs.

Doris pulled past a white building with colorfully flashing neon signs. "That's Frank Sebastian's Cotton Club," she said. "All the movie people go there to eat, dance, and be seen."

"What's it like inside, Doris?" Kiki asked eagerly.

"Are you kidding? I couldn't afford to check my coat in a joint like that."

"But you've got a job at MGM."

Doris shot Kiki a wry smile. "I'm just a production assistant. That means I'm in charge of getting coffee and sharpening pencils. But I haven't given up yet. Someday I'll land an acting job. And then who knows? You might see Doris McDougal in the Cotton Club after all."

Gosh, thought Kiki, Doris has been here a lot longer than me, but I just showed up and walked into a leading role. Somehow it seemed pretty unfair. But then everyone knew making it in acting involved a lot of luck as well as talent and skill. Kiki felt bad for Doris and hoped she'd get her big break soon. But that didn't make her own good fortune any less thrilling. Now that she had a place to sleep, the excitement of it all came rushing back.

Wouldn't it be best if I could get to the Cotton Club before Merlin whisks me back to Westdale, Kiki thought. She imagined herself stepping across the neon-lit threshold of Hollywood's fanciest club. Tingling with excitement, she realized that her daydreams were closer to coming true than they'd ever been before. By tomorrow, she'd be a star, and then the door of Frank Sebastian's would open wide for her!

As they drove through the city, Doris pointed out the famous, fashionable places to go. As they passed each one, Kiki pictured herself as the main attraction. She wished she could share her incredible soon-to-be-true daydreams with Doris. But, she hesitated, maybe the flash success story would only make her new friend feel bad. Doris had been looking for her big break for a long time, while Kiki had lucked out early. No, Kiki decided, she'd just keep the day's amazing events to herself, for Doris's sake.

Doris's voice brought Kiki back to the present—or was it the past? It was all so confusing, almost as if the whole time-trip were a script dreamed up by MGM. "Here it is," Kiki's new friend said, pulling up in front of a small cluster of tiny white bungalows. "Home sweet home."

Kiki got out of the Packard and followed Doris into one of the bungalows. The tiny room was furnished with a worn brocade sofa, a few old chairs, a low coffee table, and a rickety little dinner table. An old-fashioned radio with a framed snapshot on top of it sat near a comfortable-looking armchair. A sink and hot plate in one corner acted as the kitchen. Boy, Kiki thought, I always assumed that movie people made a lot of money. But then Hollywood hasn't turned out to be quite like I pictured it in any other way, either. And besides, Doris hasn't made it yet.

"How do you feel about franks and beans?"
Doris asked, tossing down her purse onto a
faded armchair.

For a brief moment, Kiki thought longingly of
her mother's cooking. She'd give anything for
some of Mama's stuffed cabbage right now! But
she remembered herself. If it weren't for Doris,
she thought, I wouldn't be eating anything at
all. "Sounds delicious," she said with a smile.
"Can I help you get dinner ready?"

"Nope. There's nothing too difficult about the
kind of cooking I do. Besides, the kitchen gets
crowded real easily." Doris motioned to the
cramped corner with the hot plate and sink.
"Why don't you relax a bit? I'm going to wash
up, and then I'll get dinner started."

As Doris headed for the bathroom, Kiki laid
her 1980s' clothes next to Doris's purse and sank
thankfully into another chair. She'd had a long,
hard evening in Hollywood—and to think that
she'd been through a whole day at O. Henry
High and a breakup with Steve before it!

Steve! Kiki sighed. The thing was that in a pe-
culiar way, Steve's faults were one and the same
as his good points. When half the guys on the
football team had painted their rival team's field
purple before a big game, Kiki had thanked her
lucky stars that she had a sensible boyfriend like
Steve. And the truth was, she missed him, faults
and all. And she had to admit it—she missed her
family, too. She couldn't get over the nagging
feeling that she should call her parents and let
them know she was all right. But that was silly.

Back in Westdale, less than half a minute had passed. Kiki giggled. Imagine telling Mama and Papa I'm going to be away for two days and then showing up just a little late for dinner.

Doris stepped out of the bathroom, her face scrubbed clean of all the makeup and her bleached-blond hair tied back in a ponytail. The transformation was incredible. Without the cosmetics, her natural, simple beauty could shine through. She had gentle, kind eyes, Kiki decided. She'd make a terrific romantic lead. "You look great," Kiki told her. Without her Hollywood starlet disguise, Doris didn't seem all that different from one of her friends in Westdale.

Doris laughed. "You're a funny one. Here I am without a bit of makeup on and you think I look great. Let me tell you, kid, in the past three years, no one but my mother has seen me without makeup." She walked over to the kitchen and began boiling some water for the frankfurters. Then she pulled a can of Heinz baked beans from the cupboard and began to open it with a rusty, hand-held can opener.

Kiki smiled. "Where I come from, a lot of girls don't wear any at all. You should try it sometime." She watched her friend working. Doris would flip if I sneaked an electric can opener back here from the '80s, Kiki laughed. But those Heinz beans probably taste exactly the same as they do back home. The label on the can was different but Kiki was sure the recipe hadn't changed in fifty years.

"Oh, darn," Doris exclaimed, "I just broke a nail. I think I've got a file in my purse, though."

Leaving the can of beans by the hot plate, Doris hurried over to the chair where her purse and Kiki's clothes lay.

"Say, what's this?" she asked, holding up Kiki's red jeans. "Why, Kiki, honey, it's your crazy costume from that *Flash Gordon* movie. You know you could get in a lot of trouble for taking this out of the studio!" She turned the waistline of the pants inside out. "Oh, Kiki, and you've lost the MGM costume tag. Now they'll never know where to hang it in the costume room!"

Kiki gulped. She should have known things were going too well to stay that way. "Uh, Doris, I—I have to tell you something," she said meekly. "I wasn't really working on *Flash Gordon*. Those clothes don't belong to MGM." She stopped, unsure of what to say next.

Doris just stared at her for a moment, the pants hanging limply in her hands. Then she laughed. "Oh, I get it. You decked yourself out in this ridiculous outfit so they'd let you into the studio, huh? Hoping to get lucky and meet some director or producer who'd give you an audition? It's a great idea. I wish I'd thought of it when I first got to Hollywood!"

Kiki laughed, too. "Doris, you're amazing. You've explained it all better than I could have myself!"

"So how did it go?" Doris asked, dropping the jeans, fishing for a file in her purse, and then expertly shaping the broken fingernail into a smooth arc. "Did you meet any big-time film people?"

Kiki had avoided volunteering the information so far, but she didn't want to tell Doris any more little white lies. She'd had to do enough of that to cover her time-traveling tracks. "Well, since you asked," Kiki began, "I actually did get cast in a movie!"

"You did?" Doris cried, sounding almost as thrilled at the idea as Kiki. "What part? What movie?"

"It's the *lead*, Doris, can you believe it?" Kiki couldn't keep the enthusiasm inside a second longer. "The movie's called *Stars in Her Eyes*. The star, Collette somebody-or-other, quit the picture, and the director, Marty Lester, said he'd help me become a big star!"

Doris put down the nail file and walked quickly back to the kitchen. "That's swell," she said, her tone of voice suddenly much less enthusiastic. She finished opening the can of beans and dumped them into a pot.

Oh, no. Maybe I should have kept my mouth shut after all, Kiki thought uncomfortably. She couldn't blame her new friend for being envious, she just wished her own good luck wouldn't make poor struggling Doris feel so bad.

But Doris seemed to know just what was on Kiki's mind. "I'm not jealous, kid, if that's what you're thinking," she said. "You've heard the old saying, all that glitters isn't gold. Well, that goes double for Hollywood. There's a lot of talk and a lot of hype, but sometimes the action's slow in coming. I've seen what it can do to people."

"What do you mean? Don't you think I should take the role?"

"Are you kidding? I'd kill for a part like the one you just landed. But I want you to know the sneaky kind of people you'll be working with. You've gotta be careful." Doris shrugged. "Hey, look, I don't want to take the wind out of your sails before you're even launched. Besides, I'm sure you can take care of yourself." She dished the franks and beans onto two chipped china plates and set them down on the table.

Kiki stood up and walked over. She wasn't quite sure what Doris meant. What could go wrong? Still, she didn't want Doris to think she wasn't grateful for the advice. "I promise I'll be careful," she said.

"Good. Now let's eat. I'm starved." Doris pulled up a chair and dug into the food. "After dinner, we can turn on the radio. There's a Benny Goodman concert being broadcast from the Hollywood Bowl later tonight."

"Isn't there anything good on TV?" Kiki asked, taking a bite of hot dog.

Doris looked up, confused. "TV? What's that?"

Kiki groaned inwardly. Of course, what a dumb mistake. Nobody had television sets back in 1939! "Uh, it's just the name of a local radio station we get back in Connecticut," she fudged. "I forgot you couldn't hear it out here."

"Oh," said Doris, eyeing her curiously.

Kiki glanced over at the sturdy, old-fashioned radio, which stood by the armchair, and the photo in an inexpensive gilt frame sitting on top of it. A young man in overalls smiled out of the picture.

"Who's that, Doris?" Kiki asked, pointing.

"Just an old beau," Doris replied easily. "He's still in Kansas." She turned to Kiki. "Do you have a guy?"

"Well, I used to," she said, picturing Steve's familiar face, a pang of loneliness washing through her. "But, uh, we kind of broke up before I left Connecticut." She shrugged, trying to seem less homesick than she felt. "He's a great person, but he's strictly a small-town guy. He wouldn't fit in out here at all."

"I know what you mean," Doris said. "Tommy's a farmer—a real hayseed by Hollywood standards." She sighed. "But you know, there are a lot of phonies in show business. Tommy was no movie star, but sometimes I really miss him."

"I miss Steve, too," Kiki admitted. "Sometimes I really wish we could be together." She scooped up a forkful of beans. "But then other times I'm sure we're just too different to be happy as a couple. Steve belongs in Westdale."

"And you were born to be an actress," Doris finished.

"Exactly. Landing that leading role today just proves it. Hollywood is where I belong."

"Pretty hard to live in California and be with

93

someone in Connecticut," said Doris sympathetically.

"Oh, I know some couples do live on both the East and West coasts. They fly—" Kiki interrupted herself just in time. People didn't just hop into airplanes for cross-country trips back in 1939, and they certainly didn't lead the jet-set, bicoastal life-style. Here, you'd have to spend several days and nights on a train to get from one end of the country to the other.

But Doris didn't seem to notice Kiki's gaff. "Sounds like a horrible way to live," she said, polishing off the last of the meal. "Imagine spending half the year in one place and half the year in another. It would be awful getting work. Me, I want to meet a nice, sincere guy right here in Hollywood."

"That shouldn't be too hard," Kiki said with a laugh. "I saw some real neat-looking guys around the studio today."

Doris got up to clear the table and put some water on to boil for coffee. "Good-looking, sure. Hollywood's full of lookers. But I said nice and sincere. That's the hard part. A lot of the people in Hollywood are here for one thing and one thing only—success! If you can't help them get a movie role, they don't even want to talk to you. Make one bad picture and the person you thought was your best friend runs off with your last few bucks."

"Oh, it couldn't be that bad," Kiki said easily.

"It could be and it is!" Doris insisted. "Let me tell you, Kiki, after a few more months of living in Hollywood, you'll be thrilled to find a nice steady guy like your Steve back in Connecticut."

Kiki glanced at the photo on the radio again. Thoughtfully, she studied the open, friendly face of Doris's hometown boyfriend. Steve had that same kind of look, caring and warm but not too exciting. "Don't worry, Doris. I bet you'll meet a nice guy out here," she said.

"You too, kid." Doris walked over to the radio, her gaze resting fondly on Tommy's picture for just a moment. Then she looked away quickly and flicked on the radio. "How about catching a little of that Benny Goodman concert before bed?"

"Wow!" Kiki exclaimed as the smooth, romantic music floated out of the heavy old radio. "This stuff is great!"

"What do you mean?" Doris asked curiously. "Don't tell me you've never heard Benny Goodman's orchestra? What do they play on that TV radio of yours back home?"

Nothing like this, that's for sure, Kiki thought. Somehow, she just couldn't imagine this sweet, sassy song being made into a rock video.

The old-fashioned music was soothing, and as the two friends settled into armchairs and let the sounds wash over them, Kiki suddenly felt a wonderful sense of calm. She knew she should study her lines—after all, she had fifteen pages of them to memorize before the shoot the next morning—but she figured that could wait for another half hour. She was going to be up most of the night anyway working on the script. She wanted to show everyone on that set tomorrow the most stunning and emotion-packed performance they'd seen. Kiki nibbled nervously on a fingernail.

"What's the matter, hon, getting a case of the jitters?" Doris asked softly.

Kiki sighed heavily. "Doris, do you think I can really pull this off? I mean, I'm just a nobody, and the only plays I've ever acted in were high-school productions. What if I goof up?"

Doris laughed. "Of course you can do it. Whenever you're feeling nervous, just remember that everyone was in the same boat as you are when they started out, from Collette right up to Judy Garland."

"Yeah, I guess so," Kiki said, glad that at least one of them had confidence in her. But it didn't stop her stomach from doing flip-flops. She'd been handed the chance to make all her fantasies come true, and now she had to live up to them or she'd have no one to blame but herself.

"Oh, my gosh!" Kiki cried, horrified, as she gazed at her reflection in the dressing-room mirror. "Is that really *me?*"

It had taken two whole hours for the MGM makeup people and hairstylists to transform her into the perfect star of 1939 and now Kiki was close to tears. Her straight brown hair had been cut, permed, and dyed blond. Her eyebrows had been tweezed until only two thin lines were left, then penciled in with makeup. The false eyelashes glued to her eyelids reminded her vaguely of two dead spiders, and her red lipstick was bright enough to stop traffic.

"I look like something out of *Halloween*," she moaned with dismay.

"What?" asked one of the makeup assistants.

"Never mind," Kiki muttered. The movie *Halloween* wouldn't be anyone's on-screen nightmare for several decades! Most of the actors in it weren't even born yet.

Kiki stared forlornly at herself in the mirror. Was this what Marty meant when he said they'd work on my image—that they'd make me look like the leading creep from a horror movie? Why, I barely even recognize myself. I mean, when I get back to Westdale, I'm going to have to walk around with a paper bag over my head for weeks! Tears welled up in her eyes, threatening to unstick the false lashes. She never should have signed that movie contract in Marty's office this morning.

As Kiki reached toward the cold cream and tissues, Marty stuck his head in the door. She turned to face him and he broke into a grin. "Stunning!" he exclaimed. "Absolutely stunning!"

Kiki's hand stopped in midair. "Really?" she asked, desperately wanting to believe it was true.

"Of course," Marty said. "It's exactly the image we're looking for. Very glamorous and completely up-to-date. Believe me, kid, audiences are gonna eat it up."

Kiki smiled weakly. To her, up-to-date meant designer sweatclothes and the natural look in makeup. But she was in the thirties now, not the eighties, and styles were, to say the least, quite a bit different.

"Oh, by the way, I've been thinking about your new stage name," Marty said. "How does Aileen Adair sound to you?"

Kiki frowned. She still couldn't get used to the idea of a stage name. What was so wrong with just calling herself Kiki Wykowski? Okay, it wasn't that glamorous, but she liked the way it sounded, and it had a lot of character—*her* character.

But as she glanced in the mirror, she had to admit that she'd already given up quite a bit of the old Kiki. Her real name didn't seem to fit the beauty queen of the thirties staring out at her. "Aileen Adair," she said, rolling the name off her tongue smoothly. Actually, it sounded pretty good. It was kind of exotic, as though it belonged to some rare tropical bird or something.

It might be fun to become Aileen Adair, Kiki thought. It can be like an acting role but I'll make up the script as I go along and I won't have to agonize over memorizing lines. Sure, I've even played this part before! Darling, you look gorgeous, she imagined herself saying to Ramona back in the halls of O. Henry High. But this time, the role would be for real.

"Okay, Aileen Adair it is," she said, flashing a sparkling movie-star smile at Marty.

"You're gonna knock 'em dead, Aileen," Marty told her. "Now come on. I want you to meet your costar."

Kiki pushed herself out of her chair. One of the

makeup assistants held the door open for her, and Marty led her back to the set. As the production assistant hurried past them, Marty reached out and grabbed the young woman's arm.

"Go find Kyle Kirby," he said, continuing toward where the cameras were set up, "and tell him I want to see him right away." The woman nodded easily and hurried off again.

But Kiki had stopped dead in her tracks. "Kyle Kirby!" she gasped. Why, she'd seen him in a dozen old movies! He always played a dashing, romantic character, the kind of man who had women falling all over him. And now there he was, sauntering across the set toward her, a tall, slender man with a loose, easy walk that made him look as if he had the whole world balanced on the tip of his little finger. His wavy brown hair was brushed back from his face, and his smile gleamed whiter than an Ultra Brite toothpaste commercial.

"Aileen Adair," Marty said, "I'd like you to meet Kyle Kirby."

Kyle's smile grew even wider and his sexy aquamarine eyes twinkled as he took Kiki's hand and said, "Pleased to meet you, Miss Adair. Marty has told me wonderful things about you. I'm sure working together is going to be just grand."

The touch of Kyle's hand sent shivers of excitement through Kiki's body. Her heart thudded, and her legs felt like boiled spaghetti. I'm shaking hands with a real movie star, she thought with awe. An honest-to-goodness Hollywood hero! "Hi," she murmured weakly.

"Okay," Marty broke in, "let's get to work. We've got a movie to make." He motioned toward the set, which had been arranged to look like an elegant Hollywood office. "Now the first scene I want to rehearse is the one where the two of you meet for the first time. Kyle, you'll be sitting behind the desk, working on a pile of papers. Aileen, you walk through that door"—he pointed—"and come over to the white X on the floor. Now let's run through the scene a few times before we roll the film. Places, everybody!"

Nervously, Kiki took her place out of range of the cameras.

"Action!" Marty called.

With her heart fluttering, Kiki opened the door and made her entrance. Kyle looked up from his papers, his blue-green eyes meeting hers, and his face broke into a dazzling smile. Gosh, Kiki thought dreamily, he's even more handsome in person than in the movies.

"And what can I do for you?" Kyle recited the scene's opening words.

Suddenly, Kiki's mind went completely blank. My line, she thought frantically. What's my line? Still staring into Kyle's eyes, she swallowed hard and stammered, "Uh, um, I . . ."

"Cut! Cut!" Marty shouted. "What's the problem, huh?"

"I—I am sorry," Kiki muttered. "I forgot my line."

"Hey, I'm giving you a big break here. Don't

clam up on me, kid. Now run through it again and this time, try to get the first line right!''

Kiki turned back toward the door to retrieve her script, but Kyle came around the desk and stopped her. ''You look a little nervous,'' he said with a smooth smile. ''Is everything okay?''

Being so close to Kyle made Kiki tingle all over. ''It's just . . . your eyes,'' she blurted, gazing up into them. ''I—I didn't expect them to be so blue. Back home I've only seen you in black-and-white videotapes.''

Kyle raised an eyebrow. ''Videotapes? What's that?''

Oops, Kiki thought, now how am I going to get out of this one? She improvised quickly. ''Oh, uh . . . it's just a slang word we say back in Connecticut for movies. You know, talkies, flicks, videotapes—it's all the same.''

Kyle laughed. ''You easterners sure use some funny expressions.'' He reached out and took her hand. ''You know,'' he said, ''I think we're going to get along just fine. Between you and me, I'm glad Collette's gone. She's awful when she's in a bad mood. But I can see you're not that way.'' With a teasing smile, he brushed a wisp of curly blond hair off Kiki's forehead. ''Why, I bet you haven't even been in Hollywood a month. How old did you say you were, Miss Adair?''

Kiki could feel herself blushing. Suddenly sixteen seemed much too young. Kyle had to be at least twenty-one, and he was sophisticated beyond his years. Of course, if you went strictly by birth dates, she reminded herself, he'd be half a century older than I am! Wow, talk about older men! Quickly, Kiki decided she couldn't tell him her real age or he'd never take her seriously. "I'm nineteen," she fibbed, "going on twenty."

"Young, talented, and beautiful," Kyle said smoothly. His smile seemed to sparkle like a string of rhinestones. "Miss Adair, I'm awfully glad fate has brought us together." He lifted her hand gently to his lips and brushed it with a tender kiss.

Kiki's heart seemed to skip a beat. This guy was incredible! Romantic, suave, totally gorgeous—she'd never met anyone so fantastic.

But deep down, beneath all her excitement, Kiki felt a pang of guilt. She wasn't supposed to be flirting with Kyle. How would it make Steve feel?

But Steve and I broke up. Besides, he might be A-OK back in Westdale, but Hollywood is a different world. I'm a movie star now, and I need to be with someone more similar to me. Someone like Kyle . . .

Gazing into Kyle's eyes, Kiki reminded herself that she'd really accepted two roles. The innocent young woman she played in *Stars in Her Eyes* was the easy part. But now she had to switch over to the glamorous movie star named Aileen Adair. Fluttering her false eyelashes at Kyle, she slipped quickly into the role. "I'm glad we met, too, Mr. Kirby. It's quite an honor to be working with you."

"Please," he said, "call me Kyle."

"All right, Kyle," she replied, savoring the

sound of his name on her lips. "And you can call me K— I mean, Aileen."

Kyle smiled. "Shall we run through the scene, Aileen?"

"Yes, certainly," Kiki breathed, her hand tingling from Kyle's touch.

She fumbled with her script, searching for the correct page. Maybe Aileen Adair was just a made-up name, but there was nothing phony about the way her heart was pounding. In fact, she thought, gazing into Kyle's sparkling blue eyes, I'm beginning to think Westdale was the dream all along, and that I've only just woken up to the real world called Hollywood!

Chapter Nine

"OH, DORIS, THE ABSOLUTE BEST THING happened." Kiki ran across the MGM parking lot to meet her friend after the second day of shooting *Stars in Her Eyes*. "Kyle asked me out for dinner tonight," she cried. "He's picking me up in half an hour." She pushed her bleached-blond curls out of her eyes. "We're going to this place called the Brown Derby."

"This place?" Doris stared at her. "Where did you say you were from—Mars? The Brown Derby just happens to be the most glamorous nightclub in Hollywood. All the biggest names in show business go there—not to mention every gossip columnist in town."

"Wow, you're kidding! Boy, Kyle must really like me to take me to a place like that!" But her mood took a nosedive as she grabbed the hem of her skirt. She gazed forlornly at the green-and-white-flowered dress she'd been wearing for the past two days. "Oh, no, I can't wear this outfit to a fancy club like that."

"Don't worry, kid. I've got an evening gown

you can borrow. It's no Paris original, but it'll do in a pinch."

"Doris, you're the greatest," Kiki said thankfully as they climbed into the Packard. She leaned back against the seat and sighed dreamily. "You know what Kyle told me today?" Her pulse raced just remembering his words. "'Aileen, you lovely creature, I'd rather be sitting here alone with you than with Greta Garbo, Jean Harlow, and Bette Davis combined,'" she repeated, turning to Doris. "Isn't that romantic?"

"The model gentleman," Doris said, her words tinged with more than a drop of sarcasm. She pulled out of the MGM gates onto the crowded, colorful Hollywood streets.

"Hey," Kiki asked, "did I say something wrong?"

Doris hesitated. "No," she answered gently, her voice softening. "It's just that . . . I wouldn't want you to get hurt or anything. Kyle Kirby has a reputation for . . . well, you know, with his leading ladies." She shrugged, keeping her eyes on the road. "But hey, you can't believe everything you read in fan magazines, can you?"

Kiki laughed. "You sure can't! You know there was an article about *Stars in Her Eyes* today, and it said that Marty had discovered me working as a waitress at a grimy diner outside of Los Angeles. I've never *been* to any diners since I've gotten here."

"There you go," Doris agreed, but she didn't sound convinced.

Kiki couldn't mistake the warning note in Doris's voice. But Doris couldn't be right about Kyle, could she? "You don't really think he could be using me, do you?" she asked nervously. "I mean, he seems so sincere. When we're filming, he barely takes his eyes off me, and when we're working on the love scenes he says every line as if it comes straight from his heart. He seems to care about me and . . . I think he really does . . ." Kiki's voice faded into uncertainty and disappointment.

"Hey, relax, kid," Doris said. "You're gonna have a great time tonight. To tell you the truth, I wish it were me."

"Oh, Doris," Kiki said earnestly, pushing any doubts about Kyle from her mind, "you'll get your big break soon. I just know it."

"Don't you worry about me." Doris shot Kiki one of her crooked smiles and asked, "So how'd your second day of shooting go today? You look kind of beat."

"I am," Kiki said wearily. "Getting to work at six A.M. is pretty tough, especially since I'm up half the night memorizing my lines." She sighed. "I wouldn't mind working so hard if it were all acting, but I've done so much sitting around in the last two days. You've got to wait while the crew puts up the scenery, wait while they position the cameras, and wait while they do who knows what else. Then I have to get into my costume and sit around for another half hour while the makeup people fix my face and spray gunk all over my hair. All that just so we can shoot a one-minute scene.'' She shook her head. ''I never thought making movies would be so boring!''

Doris laughed. ''This isn't Shakespeare, kiddo.'' She stopped at a red light and turned to Kiki. ''What's *Stars in Her Eyes* about, anyway?''

''The main character is a girl from Ohio—that's me—who comes to Hollywood hoping to make it big,'' Kiki explained. ''She falls in love with a producer—that's Kyle—''

''And they live happily ever after?'' Doris finished. The light turned green, and she stepped on the gas.

Kiki nodded. ''It's corny.''

''Well, they can't all be Academy Award-winners.''

''I guess not,'' Kiki conceded. ''But corny or not, I thought being in a Hollywood movie would teach me something about acting.'' She frowned. ''Turns out, I learned more from my high-school drama coach than I'm learning from Marty. Every time I ask him how he wants me to play a scene, he says the same thing: 'Give it a lot of emotion, kid, and don't flub your lines.' He never tells me what kind of emotion. And he wants me to talk in a high, breathy voice. He thinks it sounds sweet and sexy, but if you ask me, it just sounds dumb!''

''That's Hollywood,'' Doris said, giving Kiki

a sympathetic glance. "But if you want to be a star, you've got to put up with it."

"I guess so," Kiki said. "It's kind of disappointing, though. I mean, I thought I would really get to use my craft as an actress."

Doris pulled up in front of her bungalow and got out of the car. "Being a star and being a serious actress aren't always the same thing." She walked to the door, digging in her pocket for her keys. "Hey," she exclaimed, "what's this?"

A long white box was sitting on the doorstep. Kiki picked it up and read the card. "It's for me," she said with excitement. It had to be either Kyle or Marty who'd sent it. Besides Doris, they were the only people she knew in Hollywood—or in 1939, for that matter.

"Well, open it," Doris said. "Don't keep me in suspense."

Kiki picked up the box gingerly and pulled the top off. "Oh, look!" she cried breathlessly. Inside was a bouquet of long-stemmed red roses. "Ooh, they're beautiful!" she gasped. A small envelope lay tucked inside the tissue-paper cushion. She opened it and pulled out a card. "Eleven long-stemmed beauties," she read out loud. "The twelfth is you. Love, Kyle."

Doris let out a low whistle. "That Kyle Kirby can sure turn on the charm."

Kiki cradled the roses in her arms and breathed in their sweet fragrance. Last year, on Valentine's Day, Steve had given her a bouquet of daisies. Back then, Kiki had thought it was the most wonderful present in the whole world. But now . . . Well, how could daisies compare with long-stemmed roses? And how could an ordinary guy like Steve compare with a famous movie star like Kyle?

"Kyle," she whispered, savoring the sound of his name. She picked up the card and held it to her heart. Okay, she thought, maybe making a movie hasn't turned out to be quite as challenging as I expected. But who cares? I'm in Hollywood, I'm on my way to becoming a star— and tonight I'm going to the Brown Derby with the most handsome, the most sexy, the most exciting leading man in all of show business. Who could ask for anything more than that?

"Aileen," Kyle said as the chauffeur helped her into the limousine, "you are truly a vision of loveliness."

Kiki had to admit she felt pretty fantastic in the low-cut black evening gown Doris had lent her. She patted her mass of blond curls. Now if I could just get used to these garters! She took a deep breath and wiggled in her seat. I never realized what a wonderful invention pantyhose are.

Looking at Kyle, she thought, you look pretty terrific yourself. In his tuxedo, with a white silk scarf draped about his neck, Kyle was the ultimate in Hollywood suave. Not even Tom Cruise could match his startling good looks and the neon blue intensity of his eyes.

The limo took off down the street, and Kyle

opened a bottle of champagne from a silver bucket. Popping the cork deftly with one hand, he poured two glasses. "To us," he said, gallantly giving one to Kiki.

Kiki almost blurted out that she wasn't old enough to drink. But then she remembered herself. To Kyle she was nineteen, going on twenty. And a star. She had to live up to her glamorous, worldly image. With her heart fluttering, she accepted the glass and took a tentative sip. "Ooh," she gasped, "the bubbles tickle my nose!"

Kyle laughed. "Is this the first time you've ever had champagne?"

"Well . . . yes," she admitted. Except in my dreams, she added silently to herself.

Kyle put his arm around her shoulders and pulled her close. "From now on you'll have all the champagne you can drink," he said with a sexy smile. "I'll see to that."

Having Kyle so close made Kiki's pulse quicken and her insides feel like they were turning into cotton candy. As she met Kyle's enticing gaze, though, an unexpected pang of guilt shot through her. Steve! How would he feel if he could see her now? Jealous? Indifferent? Maybe even glad that her career was turning out exactly as she'd always dreamed?

Kiki sighed heavily. Probably none of those things. Practical old Steve would find some silly detail that wasn't quite perfect and use it to prove that being a star wasn't such a great idea.

Then he'd try to convince her to come back to Westdale and apply to colleges.

Compared to Kyle, Steve Goldman seemed about as exciting as a slice of Wonder Bread. She tried to imagine him drinking champagne or taking her out to dinner in a limousine, but the picture that popped into her head was just too comical to take seriously. Steve's idea of a good time was grabbing a couple of burritos at the local Mexican restaurant and then watching an old movie on TV.

Anyway, Steve and I decided to cool it for a while, Kiki reminded herself. So I'm free to date whoever I want. She took another sip of champagne and let her guilt dissolve like one of the bubbles in her drink.

"Here we are, my dear," Kyle said as the limo pulled to a stop. "The Brown Derby."

Kiki stared excitedly out the window as the chauffeur came around and opened the door of the limo. She slid out, feeling a little light-headed from the champagne. Taking a few shaky steps on the perilously high spike-heeled shoes Doris had lent her along with the dress, she almost lost her balance. But instantly Kyle was there, taking her arm and leading her under the white building's red awning. Feeling his grasp, so gentle yet so firm, Kiki almost wanted to lean over and kiss him right there in public. In his black tuxedo with the red carnation in the lapel, he was the most handsome guy she had ever seen. Wow! she thought in awe, it's really happening, just like in one of my fantasies. The stardom, the gorgeous costar, the limo—she had it all. And this time it was for real! Well . . . almost.

Stepping through the Brown Derby's double doors, Kiki felt every bit as nervous as she had the first time they'd rolled the cameras and gotten one of her performances on film. She had never been in such an elegant place before. In fact, she thought as the maître d' led them through the foyer and into the main dining room, I've never even *imagined* a place this elegant.

The room was painted red, with heavy velvet drapes and a thick, plush carpet. The tables were covered in spotless white linen and set with roses and tall red candles that matched the flowers. The gentle candlelight flickered romantically.

The Brown Derby was packed with people. A woman in a shimmering blue gown made completely of crystal beads was dining with a distinguished-looking man with a top hat and a pearl-handled cane. A group of more casually dressed young men seemed fervently engaged in a conversation. A few champagne bottles stood empty on their table. Another party was just finishing off what looked like a huge chocolate birthday cake.

As Kyle and Kiki made their way between the tables, heads began to turn. Soon, practically everyone in the room was watching them. They were a sensation. Kiki's heart was in her throat. What if she tripped or bumped into something?

But at the same time, she was absolutely thrilled to be the center of attention. Gosh, she thought, I really *am* a movie star. It was too incredible for words. With her head held high, she walked grandly across the room, feeling positively elated with each step. The maître d' led them to a cozy little table in the corner, clearly one of the Brown Derby's best.

As soon as they sat down, the room started buzzing. "Who *is* she?" Kiki heard a woman behind her whispering.

"I don't know," a man's voice said, "but she sure is a beautiful sight."

"She must be famous," another voice whispered. "After all, she's with Kyle Kirby."

Boy, thought Kiki, this is great. If only my friends could see me now! She glanced over at Kyle. He was obviously enjoying all the attention, too. Just the opposite of Steve, Kiki thought. He'd take one look at the place and try to duck out for a burger at McDonald's!

At one subtle flick of Kyle's wrist, a waiter hurried over. Talk about great service, Kiki thought. "My lovely friend and I would like some champagne before we order dinner," he said, throwing her a stunning smile. "As usual, bring the best you have."

As the waiter rushed toward the kitchen, Kyle leaned across the table. His blue-green eyes looked more brilliant than ever. "We seem to be causing quite a stir here tonight. And judging by Miss Parsons's reaction, all of Hollywood is going to know about it in the morning." He nodded toward a woman in a large yellow hat who was making a dash for the telephones.

"Who's that?" Kiki asked, barely bothering to look at the woman. Kyle's eyes were so much more interesting.

Kyle laughed. "You really are an innocent, aren't you? That's Louella Parsons, one of the hottest gossip columnists in Hollywood." He smiled with satisfaction. "We'll be in all the papers tomorrow morning. I can even give you a good idea of what they'll say—'Who was that pretty young starlet seen at the Brown Derby with Kyle Kirby last night? Inside sources tell me it's Aileen Adair, a glittering new talent that puts even Jean Harlow to shame.'"

The waiter brought the champagne, and once again there was the sound of a cork popping. Whoa, Kiki warned herself, you better go slow on this glass. She'd never had champagne back in Westdale, and she wasn't used to the alcohol. She decided to drink only half a glass more— she didn't want to miss a single thing about this wonderful evening by getting woozy.

Kyle raised his long-stemmed crystal goblet. "To the beautiful and talented Aileen Adair."

Kiki broke into a grin and took a sip of her champagne. She felt happy and carefree. What's watching TV with Steve compared to having a handsome movie star tell you you're more talented than Jean Harlow? she thought. And what's eating stuffed cabbage with your family in East Westdale compared to sipping champagne with Kyle Kirby at the Brown Derby?

Kiki just couldn't take her eyes off Kyle and he obviously had eyes only for her. There was something magical happening between them, Kiki could feel it. Kyle reached across the table and took Kiki's hand in his. "Aileen," he whispered.

"Oh, Kyle," she whispered back. Kiki felt tingly all over, as if she were made of champagne bubbles. She could barely concentrate on what Kyle was saying—something about taking her to Malibu after their nine-day intensive shooting schedule was over—because everything seemed to be fading. Maybe it's the champagne, she thought light-headedly.

Kiki raised her glass—and got the shock of her life. Her hand was nearly as transparent as the champagne! Oh my gosh, she realized, it's *me* who's fading. I'm starting to return to the present, to Westdale, to everything that's boring and dull. And Kyle—how could she possibly leave him, especially at a moment like this!

But this was no time to panic. If I don't duck out of sight right now, those gossip columnists will have a lot more to talk about than MGM bargained for!

"Kyle," she said urgently, "I have to go powder my nose. I'll be right back." Without waiting for an answer, she leapt out of her seat and half walked, half ran toward the sign that said "LADIES' ROOM."

I feel like Cinderella at the stroke of midnight,

she thought, dashing through the door. Inside, an overweight woman draped in diamonds was scrutinizing herself in the mirror. When she turned and saw Kiki, she blanched. "Oh, my goodness!" she gasped. "You're disappearing!"

"Don't worry . . . it's not catching," Kiki was unable to resist retorting. Then, without bothering to offer an explanation, Kiki ducked into one of the stalls and pulled the door shut behind her. Her fingers and toes were tingling like crazy, and she could barely feel her nose at all. Gazing down at herself, she was shocked to find that she could see right through her legs.

Wow, that was close! she breathed. Another couple of minutes and all those people out there would *really* have had something to gossip about. And poor Kyle, he'd have been stuck with the ultimate blind date . . . one that nobody could see!

Kiki giggled. Then she felt herself falling into a dark tunnel. She was being sucked back to the present. Back to Westdale. And far, far away from Kyle Kirby's tender lips.

Chapter Ten

"KIKI!" RAMONA SHRIEKED. "WHAT ON earth have you done to yourself?"

"Huh?" Kiki blinked, trying to break free of the kaleidoscope of colors that whirled around her. Though her eyes told her she was back in present-day Westdale, standing in the middle of Ashley's bedroom, her thoughts were still firmly in Hollywood, 1939. She could still see Kyle's debonair smile and feel the heart-quickening touch of his hand. "Oh, Kyle," she sighed.

"Who's Kyle?" Charmaine asked. "Come on, Kiki, snap out of it. You're back home with us now—Char and Ashley and Ramona and Lou."

"She's still confused," Ashley told the others. "It's always like that after the first time-trip."

Kiki tried to say something—anything—just to let her friends know she was okay, but her mouth refused to work. She was in the middle of a glorious dream and she didn't want to wake up. Not now. Not ever. She closed her eyes to shut out the present, trying desperately to recapture the magic feelings she'd had sitting in the Brown Derby with Kyle. She could practically see the gossip-column writers and thrilled stargazers and taste the champagne on her lips again. "Kyle!" she sighed once more.

"Never mind about Kyle, whoever *he* is," Ramona said with alarm. "What about *this*?"

Kiki felt two hands grab her shoulders. Reluctantly, she opened her eyes and found herself gazing into a mirror. Two faces stared back at her. One was Ramona's familiar face, with her straight black hair and funky pink plastic earrings. The other was a glamorous movie star with platinum bleached-blond hair, pencil-thin eyebrows, ruby red lips . . .

Slowly it began to sink in. My forty-eight hours in Hollywood are over, she thought reluctantly. No more leading role, no more dinners at fancy clubs. Her dreams were disappearing out from under her, just like they always had. Kiki groaned with frustration. I'm back in Westdale, right where I started. And what's more, I'm going to look like a real weirdo here with my 1939 makeover. She remembered how her new look had seemed to her at first glance. She'd gotten used to it—she even liked it now—but back in Westdale she was going to seem awfully strange.

"You aren't going to go to school like that, are you?" Ramona demanded.

"School?" Kiki said uncertainly. Right now O. Henry High seemed as distant as the North Pole.

"Never mind about how you look," Charmaine broke in. "Just tell us what happened. How did it feel? What did you do?"

118

"You still look kind of flipped out," Lou said. "Maybe you better sit down first."

Flipped out is right! Kiki thought groggily. She dropped onto Ashley's bed and looked around the room. How can it be true that only a couple of minutes have passed? she wondered. I feel like I've been gone for years! She glanced at her friends. They were all staring at her as if she'd just appeared from outer space. Well, she thought, that's just about how I feel!

"Listen, you guys, I'm starring in a movie," Kiki told her friends dreamily. She could picture the busy soundstage where *Stars in Her Eyes* was being filmed. "And you'll never believe who my costar is—Kyle Kirby!"

"That name sounds familiar," Ashley said. "Is he famous?"

"Sure he is," Lou replied, reaching for a potato chip. "I've seen him on TV. He was in some of those old movies."

TV? Old movies? To her friends, Kiki realized, Kyle Kirby was just a name from the distant past. But to her he was the gorgeous, suave, positively perfect guy she'd been talking and laughing with only a few minutes ago.

"Is that why you're wearing all that makeup?" Ramona asked. "For the movie?"

"No way," Kiki replied, starting to feel exasperated with how little her friends seemed to understand. "The blond hair was for the movie, but the makeup was for my date with Kyle. When I disappeared, we were at the Brown Derby, drinking champagne and—"

"Uh-oh, you're in trouble. That bleached-blond hair and tweezed eyebrows are gonna take months to grow back in," Ashley groaned.

"Wait'll the kids at school see you," Ramona added.

"The kids at school?" Kiki echoed, panic surfacing in her words. How was she supposed to go back to life at O. Henry High after being a Hollywood celebrity? All she wanted was to press Merlin's "execute" button again and— Of course! The solution was as crystal clear as the goblet she'd been drinking out of at the Brown Derby. "You have to send me back," she told Ashley.

Ashley groaned, tucking a strand of red hair behind her ears. "I can't say I didn't expect this, but Kiki, it may be best for you to leave the past where it belongs."

Lou nodded, a wise expression on her round race. "Yeah, sometimes the past can start seeming more real than the present." She reached for the potato chips.

"But I've got to get back," Kiki protested. "I'm in the middle of—"

"—your dinner with that Kyle guy?" Ramona finished for her.

Kiki looked around at her friends' anxious faces. She was going to have to come up with a better reason than just an unfinished date to convince them to send her back.

"You know, Kiki, now that you've returned to Westdale, he's at least fifty years too old for you," Charmaine reminded her gently. "He's part of another world."

And so am I, Kiki thought to herself. *A world where I'm everything I ever dreamed of being.* "Listen," she pleaded, "I've still got seven days of shooting left on the movie."

"Well . . ." Ashley shrugged her slender shoulders.

"You don't want me to fink out on my responsibilities, do you?" Kiki prodded. "And just think how good it will be for my acting to star in a real movie. What better experience could I have? It might even help me get the right start on my career back here in the present."

Deep down, a tiny voice nagged at her. She was getting more performance experience just by pretending to be a movie star in the thirties than by acting in Marty's film. But her friends were nodding in approval now, and that was what really counted.

"So you'll send me back?" Kiki asked, relief flooding through her like a stream after a spring thaw.

"I guess." Ashley stretched her lanky frame out on her four-poster bed. "But just until you finish the movie."

"Great, well, I'm due on the lot at six o'clock tomorrow morning, and I haven't even started memorizing my lines yet, so beam me down, Ashley." Kiki giggled.

Ashley and Lou exchanged glances. "But don't you remember?" Ashley said. "You can't go back for another forty-eight hours."

"Forty-eight hours!" Kiki gasped.

"Don't worry," Ashley added. "To the people

121

you left behind, it will seem like only two minutes have passed."

"Don't worry!" Kiki wailed. Her relief vanished. She was really going to have to live in the present, at least for another two days. Aileen Adair had evaporated like a dream in someone's imagination, leaving plain old Kiki Wykowski—a high-school junior at O. Henry High and part-time counter worker at Nick's Deli—in her place.

How awful, Kiki wanted to scream. It's going to be so *dull* after the amazing adventure I've been through! She tried to see herself in the hallways of O. Henry High. But the picture just didn't seem to fit anymore. She had no idea how she was going to get through even one boring day of Mrs. Killington's history class and chitchatting in the cafeteria. But she'd have to. There was no way back to the past, at least not for another two days.

Face it, Kiki told herself, you're stuck! Stuck with O. Henry High instead of MGM Studios, and the school cafeteria instead of the Brown Derby, and a high-school production of *The Pirates of Penzance* instead of a real Hollywood movie.

The panic rose in her throat again. I have to get out of here, Kiki thought frantically. Back to 1939. Back to Kyle . . .

She gazed around the room at her friends' anxious faces and moaned. "What am I going to do?"

Walking down the main hall of O. Henry High, Kiki reached up and adjusted the black scarf that covered her head. I hope none of my blond curls are showing, she thought nervously. She pushed her oversized sunglasses onto the bridge of her nose. She was wearing them to hide her plucked eyebrows but they kept sliding off. If anyone sees my face like this, they'll flip, she told herself, just like Ramona did. Just like Mama and Papa did.

Kiki winced, remembering the night before. Mama had taken one look at her and gasped, "Kiki, what in the world has happened to you?"

Seeing the horrified expression on Mama's face had brought Kiki down to earth with a thud. Thinking fast, she had come up with a feeble excuse—the Bridgeport Community Theater was putting on a production of *Private Lives*, and her new look was supposed to help her land a part.

"Acting in school plays is one thing," Papa had said. "But you don't have time to travel back and forth to Bridgeport. You've got to concentrate on your schoolwork so you can get into a good college."

"Let's just hope your eyebrows and hair grow in fast," Mama had added. "That blond color makes you look awful."

As Kiki walked down the hallway toward Mrs. Killington's history class, she tucked her books under her arm and let out a ragged sigh. Back in 1939, she told herself, no one thought I looked awful. Marty said I was stunning, and Kyle said I looked prettier than Jean Harlow. Even Doris thought I looked terrific.

123

"Nice outfit, Kiki. Are you practicing to be a fashion model or something?"

Kiki's thoughts were interrupted by Clarissa "The Mouth" Van Dyke—the biggest gossip in the junior class. Oh, great, Kiki thought. Clarissa can sniff out trouble faster than a bloodhound. "Uh, I'm late for Mrs. Killington's class, Clarissa. I don't have time to talk," she said.

"No problem, I'm walking in that direction, anyway," Clarissa replied, falling into step beside Kiki. "So come on, why are you wearing those sunglasses?"

"I went to the eye doctor this morning," Kiki lied, "and he put drops in my eyes. I have to keep the light out of my eyes for a few days."

"Oh, I see," Clarissa said, scrutinizing Kiki closely. She reached up and flicked a tiny curl that had escaped from under Kiki's scarf. "Is that blond hair I see?" she asked with interest.

Kiki felt her cheeks growing hot. "No, of course not," she muttered.

Clarissa leaned close. "By the way," she asked confidentially, "is it true you and Steve broke up?"

"That's none of your business," Kiki snapped.

Clarissa smiled smugly. "That's all I wanted to know." She gave the blond curl another flick and strode off down the hallway.

Darn that girl, Kiki thought angrily, tucking the stray hair back under the scarf. She hurried into her history class and sat down at her desk, but Clarissa's words still echoed in her head. "Is it true you and Steve broke up?" Well, is it?

she wondered. The relationship was on hold, she knew that much, but was it really over?

Kiki frowned. Meeting Kyle had changed a lot of things for her—she'd felt important and glamorous when they were together. He was so exciting, so sophisticated—everything she'd always missed in Steve. And yet being with him hadn't made her forget her hometown boyfriend back in Westdale.

Dating Kyle had only made Kiki that much more confused, pulled between the image of the star she was becoming and the girl from Connecticut she'd always been. Kiki still hadn't sorted out her feelings about Steve. She wondered if his feelings for her were any clearer. How would he act toward her now that they'd decided to cool their relationship? Well, she'd find out today. It would be their first meeting since their conversation at the wishing well, though of course for Steve only one evening had passed.

Kiki sighed. The thing was, she missed Kyle a whole lot more than she missed Steve. She pulled her scarf down over her ears and tried to ignore the curious stares of her classmates as they walked into the room. I have to stop thinking about Kyle, she told herself. Here in the '80s, he's an old man, old enough to be my grandfather. He's a movie star from fifty years in the past. I've got to get used to what really exists now.

But it was easier said than done. Kyle was so real to her. She sighed. Those two days *had* happened. Even if they were all a fantasy, she knew nothing could compare with the thrill of sitting in the Brown Derby and hearing people whisper, "She's with Kyle Kirby. She *must* be famous." Kiki chewed on the end of her pencil. Just forty-eight hours, she sighed, and I'll be back in his arms again . . .

Mrs. Killington strode into the classroom, a sour expression on her face, her orthopedic shoes squeaking on the floor. "Miss Wykowski," she said, closing the door with a click, "I do not allow sunglasses in class. Please take them off."

With a start, Kiki's hand went up to her glasses. Oh no, she thought nervously. What am I going to do? If I don't take these off, I'll get in trouble with Mrs. Killington, but if I do, the whole class will laugh at my plucked eyebrows. The thought of everyone seeing her looking so ridiculous—by 1980s' standards, anyway—was just too awful to consider. "Um, well, the eye doctor told me I have to wear them," she said nervously.

Mrs. Killington walked down the aisle until she was standing directly in front of Kiki. "Oh, I see," she said. "Then of course you have a note from your doctor." She thrust out a gnarled hand.

Kiki's mind went blank with panic.

"Uh, no," she muttered finally, "I mean, well, I did, but I . . . must have lost it."

The evidence sounded lame even to her own ears, and judging from Mrs. Killington's expression it hadn't gone over very well with her teacher, either.

"Well then just make sure you bring another

note tomorrow," Mrs. Killington replied tartly, returning to her desk.

Kiki sighed with relief, then spent the rest of the period wondering how to forge a note from a fictitious eye doctor. Boy, Ashley was right when she warned that time-traveling could have some unexpected side effects!

When the bell finally rang, Kiki hurried out into the hall, hoping to avoid any more questions from the other kids. Clutching her books to her chest, she rounded the corner.

Steve's mop of blond hair caught her eye immediately. She stopped in her tracks, her mouth as dry as cotton. He was coming right toward her.

Now what, Kiki wondered, Steve's familiar stride bringing him close. She knew the confrontation wasn't going to be easy and she'd been hoping to put it off at least until lunchtime. Well, it looked as though it was going to happen a little sooner than she'd planned.

"Steve!" Kiki exclaimed. She looked into his familiar face and smiled uncertainly. Her heart kicked into high gear. Despite everything that had come between them, she felt ridiculously happy to see him.

"Hi," he said. His light blue chambray shirt, she observed, was the exact shade of his eyes. His sun-streaked blond hair was tousled, and Kiki had to fight the urge to smooth it back from his forehead. Funny, she'd never felt that way with Kyle, but maybe that was because Kyle was so perfect she couldn't imagine his hair ever being out of place.

127

"I'm practicing to be a movie star," she laughed, seeing the curiosity in his face as he stared at her new look. She was hoping a joke would make it seem less dreadful, but Steve wasn't laughing. "Well, I don't want to hang you up—I'm sure a movie star has better things to do than stand around talking to a nobody," he replied with a dry little smile. "Anyway, I've gotta get to class. Catch you later, Kiki." With a casual wave, he turned and hurried off down the hall.

Kiki stared after him for a moment, fighting back tears. She felt as if she'd been slapped in the face. Steve *hated* her. Either that or he was very, very hurt. But either way, it was pretty obvious that he didn't want to have anything to do with her. He'd run away from her so fast that he could have won an Oscar for fastest brush-off of the year.

Kiki bit a fingernail, feeling confused and angry. I guess I miss Steve more than I thought, she realized sadly. But he sure didn't act like he missed me. Suddenly the anger won out over the confusion. Just because we've decided to cool off our relationship a little bit doesn't mean he has to avoid me like I have a contagious disease! Kiki turned, kicking the toe of her Reeboks against the floor, and started miserably off toward her locker.

"Hey, wait up," she heard a voice call. Kiki looked up to see pint-sized Tina Scott hurrying down the hall. "I heard you had some adventure last night," Tina whispered eagerly. "It sounds so exciting! I can't believe you actually

got a leading part in a movie! And that Kyle guy
. . ." Her voice trailed off as she stared at Kiki.
"Are you okay? You look like you just lost your
best friend."

"I feel that way, too," Kiki said unhappily. "I
ran into Steve, and he couldn't get away from
me fast enough."

"Poor Kiki," Tina said sympathetically.
"What happened?"

Kiki managed a weak smile. When it came to
romance, there was no one better to confide in
than Tina Scott. Tina was an incurable romantic
and matchmaker. And as her closest friends
knew, she was also "Dear Dolly," the anony-
mous writer of the school paper's advice-to-the-
lovelorn column.

Tina linked her arm with Kiki's and steered her
toward the lockers. "Well," Kiki began, "it all
started last night. Only for me, it was three nights
ago because of the two days I spent in Hollywood." She recounted the whole conversation at
the wishing well with Steve. "So it looks like
Steve and I are splitting up, at least for the time
being. And the thing is," she finished, "sometimes I'm sure I want to end things with Steve
once and for all. But then other times, I think I'll
go crazy if I can't be with him, you know?"

Tina let go of Kiki's arm and fiddled with her
locker. "I know exactly what you mean," she
said, nodding. "And I think you need to try
dating some other guys. That way you'd know
for sure, one way or the other, if you were
meant to be with Steve."

129

"Well, maybe," Kiki began. She glanced mischievously at Tina. "Actually, I did meet this really fantastic guy . . ." She could picture Kyle's handsome face smiling sexily.

"Great," Tina said enthusiastically. "Is he from O. Henry or does he go to another school?" She pulled open her already full locker and shoved a few more books into it.

"School? Tina, I'm talking about Kyle!" Kiki exclaimed. The thought of her sophisticated movie star hanging around the halls of O. Henry High was just too much.

"Oh, Kiki, no," Tina cried, her enthusiasm turning instantly to dismay. "*Don't* fall in love with a guy from the past. I've done it, and I'm telling you, it's worse than anything in the whole world!"

Kiki stared at her friend. Obviously, Tina's adventure in the past had been pretty romantic, too.

"When I had to return to the present forever," Tina continued, "I felt like part of my whole soul was being left behind with the guy I loved. I thought the only way I'd ever get my heart back was to travel back to Nevada in eighteen ninety-two. But I couldn't keep living in the past. And you can't, either, you know. At some point, you have to accept the fact that you belong here, no matter how much you want to keep the fantasy alive!"

Kiki leaned heavily against her locker. She didn't want to hear what Tina was saying. It could be different for her and Kyle. She was sure of it.

"Look," Tina was saying, "go back to the thirties, have a great time. You can even date this Kyle person. Just don't get involved emotionally. Believe me, I know what I'm talking about."

"But Kyle's the only guy I'm interested in besides Steve," Kiki answered weakly.

"Well then you'll just have to meet some new ones. And I've got a fantastic way for you to do it." She slammed her locker shut. "The 'Hello, Dolly' Dance."

"Oh, your big matchmaking party," Kiki said with a smile.

Everyone at school knew about the dance, which the *O. Henry Herald* was sponsoring later in the month. Anyone interested could fill out one of Dear Dolly's questionnaires about their likes and dislikes, hobbies and interests. Then Tina and her boyfriend, J. C. McCloskey, were going to use Ashley's computer to match up perfect couples. Of course, the whole school would be invited to the dance. But none of the kids who'd filled out questionnaires would know who their dates were until they got to the dance.

"You've got to admit, it's a great way to meet someone," Tina laughed. "Now all you have to do is fill out a questionnaire and see who you get matched up with. You never know," she added with a grin, "you might end up with Mr. Right."

"I'm not sure," Kiki began. She couldn't imagine having a very good time with some ordinary high-school boy, not after being with a guy like Kyle.

131

"Well, it's worth a try," Tina insisted. "What have you got to lose? Besides, it really might help you find out for sure if you're in love with Steve."

"Well . . . okay," Kiki gave in reluctantly. "I'd like to have a date for the dance, and it sure doesn't look like Steve's going to ask me. I guess there's no reason not to do it." She frowned. Kiki didn't want to insult Tina, but she was certain the whole dance would seem kind of silly after getting a taste of Hollywood nightlife.

"Great," Tina said, tucking her notebook under her arm and stepping away from the locker. "Stop by the *Herald* office after school and pick up the issue with the questionnaire in it. You won't regret it, I promise." She gave a little wave and hurried down the hall to her next class.

Kiki watched her friend disappear into the crowd. If only everything were as easy as Tina made it sound. But there was just no way Dear Dolly was going to match her up with someone so wonderful he'd make her forget both Steve *and* Kyle. A guy like that simply didn't exist, at least not in Westdale.

And as for dating people other than Steve, well, she was already doing that. And no matter what Tina warned her, she and Kyle were serious about each other. When she got back to 1939, she intended to spend a lot of time with him. Because Kiki Wykowski, alias Aileen Adair, was in love with Kyle Kirby. For better or worse. And no one, not Steve or Tina or anybody else, could change it.

Chapter Eleven

"HEY, MARILYN!" J. C. McCLOSKEY CALLED as Kiki walked into school the next morning.

"Are you talking to me?" Kiki asked uncertainly.

"Yeah," J. C. replied with a grin. "You're Marilyn Monroe, aren't you?"

"Can I have your autograph?" Chuck Norwicki cried, pretending to faint dead away.

Kiki's cheeks were burning with embarrassment. She knew J. C. and Chuck were only kidding and that they didn't mean to make her feel bad. She knew she should just laugh the whole thing off. But somehow she couldn't. Back in the '30s, people were so different. When she'd walked through the door of the Brown Derby with Kyle that night half a century ago, everyone had stopped and stared—and not because they thought she looked funny, either. They knew she was someone special—a real Hollywood movie star.

Ignoring her friends' teasing, Kiki pretended she was walking into the Brown Derby right now. With her head held high, she marched grandly down the hall to her locker.

But as the day wore on, the jokes and nasty comments got harder to ignore. Carrying her tray through the lunch line, Kiki heard someone behind her whisper, "Just because she's starred in a couple of school plays doesn't mean she's so important."

"No, but I guess *she* thinks she is," another voice said. "Just look at those sunglasses. You'd think she was Madonna or something."

"Really. And Clarissa told me she dyed her hair blond, too. I mean, gimme a break!"

Kiki wished she could melt into O. Henry High's linoleum floor, like the wicked witch of the west in *The Wizard of Oz*. Instead, she squared her shoulders and pretended she hadn't heard a word. She searched around for a friend to eat with. Please, she prayed, don't make me have to sit alone. Not today. Thankfully, she spotted Ramona's dark, straight hair and hurried over to join her.

"Everybody's bugging me about the scarf and sunglasses," Kiki complained as she sat down. "I know it's stupid, but it's really starting to get to me."

"Maybe you should dye your hair back to its regular color," Ramona suggested. "At least then you wouldn't have to wear that scarf."

"No way," Kiki said irritably. "Tonight I'll be back in Hollywood, and tomorrow we've got a lot of filming to do for *Stars in Her Eyes*. I've got to look this way for the movie. And my career is a lot more important than what a bunch of dumb teenagers think."

134

"Your career?" Ramona repeated. "But that movie you're making is in the past. What about your life right here?"

"Who cares about right here?" Kiki snapped. "In nineteen thirty-nine I'm a movie star. That's all that matters now."

Ramona looked hurt, but Kiki pretended not to notice. She doesn't understand, she told herself. No one does. At least, no one in the present. But back in 1939, it's different. There, everyone knows what it means to have a star on your door and a movie contract in your hand. She forced her face into a mask of careless indifference and jabbed her fork into the soggy mass of spaghetti and meatballs on her plate.

Yet inside, Kiki felt anything but indifferent. All day long people had been putting her down. Now one of her best friends was giving her a hard time. It hurt, because even though Kiki's heart was in Hollywood in 1939, she really did care about her friends and family here. But they didn't seem to care too much about her.

She swirled her fork in her spaghetti. I wish I could just stand up and tell everyone the truth—that MGM dyed my hair and plucked my eyebrows for my role in *Stars in Her Eyes*. She laughed harshly. Sure, why not? I'll just get up and tell them I'm a big movie star back in 1939. So what if everyone thinks I'm out of my mind. She threw her fork down and pushed the tray away from her. "This stuff tastes awful," she grumbled. She took a long sip of milk and got up to leave.

"Hey, Kiki," Ramona said with concern, "are you okay?"

Kiki just shrugged. Ramona doesn't understand what it's like to go back in time because she's never done it. She probably thinks it's all fun and games, kind of like being able to walk into your favorite movie for a few hours and then walk out again and forget all about it.

Oh, well, she told herself. Who cares what people think? Tonight I'll be back in 1939, and I'll have missed only two minutes of my dream-come-true. All I have to do is make it through a few more hours in Connecticut, and I'll be a movie star again. With dreams of Hollywood running through her head, Kiki turned her back on Ramona and walked away.

"Kiki," Mama said as Kiki walked into the deli that afternoon, "come into the office. I want to talk to you."

Kiki frowned, wondering what was going on. "But who's going to watch the store?" she asked. "Is Papa upstairs?"

"Papa's making a delivery," Mama said. "Never mind the store. This is more important."

More important than the store? Kiki could hardly believe her ears. Her parents put their whole heart and soul into Nick's Deli. Whatever her mother had to say, it must be serious. "What's wrong?" she asked anxiously, following Mama into the office.

"Just this," Mrs. Wykowski said, picking up

a pile of torn papers from the desk and handing them to Kiki.

Kiki swallowed hard. Mama was holding the college applications she had ripped up and thrown in the trash yesterday afternoon. "Mama—" Kiki began, but she stopped when she saw a tear slide down her mother's cheek. She felt horribly ashamed, as if it were her mother's heart she'd torn into little bits.

"Ever since you were born, your papa and I have worked hard and saved so we could send you to college," Mrs. Wykowski said sadly. "Now what are you telling us? You don't want to go?"

Kiki didn't know what to say. If she told the truth, it would break her mother's heart. But a lie would only get her deeper into the mess. For a long moment she just stood there, paralyzed by indecision. She wanted to tell the truth, but she felt so guilty.

Yet at the same time, Kiki resented her mother for making her feel so awful that she was almost ready just to give in and go to college. What right do Mama and Papa have to force their values on me? she thought angrily. It's my life, and if I want to be an actress, I'll be one! "I've been trying to tell you for months," she said at last, "but you don't want to listen. I've decided not to go to college. I'm going to be an actress."

"An actress?" Mrs. Wykowski looked confused. "You mean an acting teacher, like the young woman who runs your Drama Club at

137

school? But Kiki, you have to go to college to do that.''

"Not an acting teacher," Kiki explained. She was trying her hardest to be patient, but she couldn't keep a bitter note of frustration out of her voice. "An actress. In the movies. I'm going to be a movie star.''

"What's this I hear about movie stars?" Papa's jovial voice cut in. He strolled through the back door, carrying the evening paper. "Has Elizabeth Taylor stopped by for a pastrami sandwich, perhaps?" But then he saw the tears on his wife's face. "What's happened?" he asked anxiously.

"Nothing," Kiki said, trying to ignore how guilty she felt. "I just told Mama I'm not going to college, that's all.''

"She ripped up the applications," Mama said, her voice cracking with emotion. "I found them in the wastebasket in her room.''

"What?" Papa cried. "Why on earth did you do that?''

"Because I want to be an actress," she answered defiantly.

Papa looked confused. "So? You're acting in plays now, and that doesn't keep you from going to high school. Why should it interfere with college?''

"You don't understand," Kiki cried, her voice rising along with her frustration. She felt pulled in two directions—loving her parents and wanting to make them happy, and fulfilling her dream. "To you, my acting is just some fun little hobby, like Jenna's stamp collection or Mimi's kids' play group at the Y. But I'm serious. I'm going to devote my whole life to acting. And as soon as I'm out of high school, I'm going to Hollywood," she finished passionately.

"Hollywood!" Papa cried. His face was tense with fury. "Absolutely not. I forbid it. You will go to college and get an education. Why do you think I left Poland to come to America? For my children's sakes. Because here a child does not have to go to work at age sixteen. Here you can make something of yourself, but you have to go to college and get an education first."

Mrs. Wykowski was sobbing openly now.

Mr. Wykowski walked over and put his arm around his wife. "What can you expect?" he said soothingly. "She's just a child. She needs us to guide her in the right direction."

"I am not a child!" Kiki shouted, tears of frustration stinging her eyes. "Please . . . can't you try to see it my way?"

But one look at their faces told her that was impossible. The hurt in their eyes made her want to crawl into a hole and hide, or run away—back to Hollywood, back to Kyle and Doris and Marty. Back to 1939.

A spark of joy lit up deep inside Kiki as she realized that she could. She'd been planning to wait until after dinner to go over to Ashley's house. But now the thought of spending even one more minute with her parents seemed unbearable.

The two days of waiting are over! I'm going

over to Ashley's right now. Not caring anymore about anything except pushing Merlin's magical button, she turned and hurried out of the office.

"Kiki!" Mama cried. "Where are you going?"

"Young lady," Papa demanded, "come back here at once!"

But Kiki wasn't about to stop now. Running up to her room, she dug into the back of her closet, grabbed Doris's black evening gown and high heels, which she had worn to the Brown Derby, and stuffed them into a large canvas bag. As she stepped back into the hallway, she found Mimi standing outside her room, an expression of unhappy confusion on her face.

"Kiki," Mimi asked, "why are Mama and Papa so mad? What did you do?"

The look on her sister's face made Kiki's heart ache. She wanted to comfort her, but how could she possibly explain what was happening? "It's nothing," she said. "Go back in your room and play. Dinner will be ready soon."

Wiping the tears from her cheeks, Kiki turned from her sister and walked down the stairs. Mr. Wykowski was behind the counter of the deli waiting on a customer. From inside the office, Kiki could just make out the sounds of her mother's heartfelt sobs. She knew she should go in and comfort her, but what could she say? Like everyone else in the present, she thought, Mama just doesn't understand. She shook her head sadly. She never has, and she never will.

Kiki grabbed her winter coat from the peg in the hallway and slipped out the front door before her parents could see her. Outside, the air was cold, and a layer of slushy snow covered the sidewalk. A few early commuters strode down the street, their heads down, their coats buttoned against the icy wind. But the winter chill didn't bother Kiki at all. In just a few minutes, she'd be in California enjoying the benefits of a year-round summer. Mmm. She could almost feel the warm breeze already.

Glancing down the street, Kiki saw her bus pulling up at the corner bus stop. Breaking into a run, she caught up with it and jumped on just before the doors closed. As the bus pulled down the street, she flopped into an empty seat and let out a relieved sigh. Soon she'd be half a century away from here. And once she was there, she was certain everything was going to be just fine.

Chapter Twelve

"OUCH!" KIKI CRIED AS ONE OF THE makeup assistants came dangerously close to her eye with a charcoal pencil. She was sitting in her dressing room while a bevy of professional cosmeticians worked on her face. A week had passed since her evening with Kyle at the Brown Derby. Since her first time-trip, she'd been back to Hollywood two more times, for a grand total of six days of living in 1939.

"Sorry, Miss Adair," one of the assistants said. "We're almost finished."

Kiki yawned and resigned herself to a few more minutes of boredom. Putting on makeup for the camera always took so long she could barely sit through it. Gosh, I'm tired, she thought. These past two weeks of jumping between Hollywood in 1939 and Westdale in the 1980s have been totally crazy. She closed her eyes and let her thoughts drift. In present-day Westdale, life was still the pits. The kids at school had grown tired of teasing her and now they just ignored her. Of course, it's not like I don't have any friends, she reminded herself.

There's still Ramona, and Charmaine, Ashley, Tina, and Lou. But even they're getting a little tired of listening to me rave about my adventures as a Hollywood star. To them I'm just plain old Kiki Wykowski. They don't really believe that in 1939 I'm a celebrity.

Kiki opened her eyes and watched the cosmeticians at work. *If only Mama and Papa could see me now. They think I need to go to college to get a good job. But just look at me. I'm not even out of high school, and I'm already starring in a Hollywood film.*

But as far as Mama and Papa were concerned, Kiki's acting career was nothing more than a foolish dream. Ever since her mother had found the ripped-up college applications, her home and the deli had become like a battlefield. Every conversation, no matter how trivial, turned into an argument about college. Then Papa would start yelling, Mama would begin to cry, and Kiki would feel so guilty she could hardly stand it. Now, just thinking about it, her eyes filled with tears. But she refused to cry. Smearing her makeup now would be disastrous.

"All set, Miss Adair," one of the makeup assistants broke into her thoughts. She held up a mirror for Kiki's approval.

At the sound of the young woman's voice, all of Kiki's bad thoughts melted away. Just hearing that name made her feel special. Blotting her lips on a tissue, she left the dressing room and hurried over to the set. It was time for her big love scene with Kyle—take sixteen. They'd started filming yesterday afternoon, but thanks to a series of flubbed lines, broken microphones, and script changes, they were still working on it today.

"Hey, kid, have you seen this?" Marty was walking toward her with a newspaper in his hand. "You made the columns again."

Kiki took the paper and quickly read through Louella Parsons's gossip column. *Debonair leading man Kyle Kirby has been painting the town red with new MGM star, Aileen Adair. Last night, Miss Adair and her famous boyfriend were spotted at the Coconut Grove, sipping champagne under the stars.*

Kiki frowned. It's weird, she thought, but whenever I hear the word boyfriend, I think of Steve. But that was all over. During the last week in Westdale, she and Steve hadn't said a word to each other. Somehow I never figured it would end like this, she thought sadly. I always imagined that even if we broke up, we'd always be friends.

Marty took the paper from Kiki and folded it under his arm. "You've been in the gossip columns every day this week," he said with satisfaction. "With all this publicity, this film is bound to be a smash."

Kiki smiled and forced Steve out of her mind. Who cares what's going on in Westdale? she thought. I'm in Hollywood now, and none of those other things are even going to happen for another half a century.

While Marty went to supervise the cameraman, Kiki collapsed into a chair and fanned herself with a script. "Whew!" she muttered. Lit by the powerful movie lights, the closed set was like an oven. And this costume, she thought with dismay—if the girdle were any tighter, I could probably fit into a size three dress!

"Well, hello there," Kyle said, emerging from his dressing room and walking over to join Kiki. "Hot, isn't it? Reminds me of the time I was in Mexico, doing a film with Merle Oberon. It must have been a hundred and ten." He pulled up a chair next to Kiki. "How does my hair look?" he asked. "It's got to be just right for this love scene."

"It's perfect," Kiki said flatly. She wasn't sure why, but over the last few days, some of the things Kyle said were beginning to annoy her. For one thing, he sure liked to talk about himself a lot.

Kiki sighed. It's probably not Kyle at all. I'm just tired because I'm leading this crazy double life, split between being a movie star and a regular old high-school kid. I shouldn't take it out on Kyle.

Still, Kiki's mind drifted back to the days when she and Steve were first falling in love. We had so many great talks together, she remembered. I could trust him with all my most secret hopes and dreams.

Kyle reached for Kiki's hand. "Aileen," he said, flashing one of his sexiest smiles, "you look absolutely breathtaking." His eyes caught hers in a passionate gaze.

Kiki let out a deep breath. It was so confusing. One moment she was thinking about Steve and the next she had eyes only for Kyle. And even more confusing than that, Kiki was beginning to realize that she didn't feel completely comfortable with either one of them. But she did know one thing for sure as she stared into Kyle's face—her costar was gorgeous.

So I haven't confided in him the way I did with Steve. But I don't need to. Because here, all my dreams are true, and Kyle understands them by living them out himself. If something between us is missing, it's probably my fault for having to keep half my life secret from him.

"Okay, folks," Marty called, "quiet on the set! Aileen, Kyle, let's try the love scene one more time."

Kiki and Kyle walked onto the set—a park bench and a couple of phony trees in front of a city backdrop—and took their places. "How should I play this scene, Marty?" Kiki asked. "It seems to me I should act sort of shy but sti—"

"Just ham it up," Marty broke in. "And don't blow your lines."

Kiki rolled her eyes. Sometimes she wondered if Marty knew how to say anything else. *He doesn't care how convincing my performance is, as long as it's romantic and mushy. This isn't acting,* she thought with frustration. *A wooden dummy could play this role!*

But then Kyle caught her eye and whispered, "Forget about acting. Right now, it's just you and me."

Kyle's smile and his tender tone made Kiki go weak with anticipation. It was in this scene that they finally confessed their love for each other— and sealed it with a kiss. And Kiki intended to enjoy every moment of it.

146

"Ready!" Marty shouted. "Lights . . . camera . . . action!"

Kiki took a deep breath and began. "I guess you think I'm just a bratty kid from Ohio," she said to Kyle.

"You bet," replied Kyle, putting his hand under her chin and tilting her head up toward him. "But you're the prettiest brat this hardened Hollywood producer has ever laid his eyes on."

It was only a line from the script, but looking into Kyle's eyes, Kiki felt her heart go into overdrive. "But Jack," she breathed, "I thought—"

"*That's* your problem, kid. Too much thinking and not enough feeling." Kyle put his arms around her and pulled her close. Their lips were only inches apart, just seconds away from a kiss.

Oh, Kyle, Kiki thought, I love you. I—

"Cut!" Marty yelled. "Who let that fleabag in here?"

Kiki let go of Kyle and turned around. A skinny calico cat had wandered onto the set. Why, she looks like Oz! she thought, kneeling down to pet her.

But before she could get near the cat, Kyle jumped toward it, shouting. "Oh, shoot! That scene was going perfectly. Get out of here, you mangy thing! Scat!" Lifting his heavy, old-fashioned shoe, he gave the cat a swift kick. The creature let out a howl and disappeared behind the scenery.

Kiki could barely believe her eyes. "Kyle!" she cried with horror, "how could you kick that poor, defenseless little cat?"

147

"Oh, come on," Kyle laughed. "Who cares about that filthy stray? Now let's hurry up and finish the scene."

"Not until I make sure you didn't hurt that cat," Kiki said unyieldingly.

Ignoring the protests of Marty and the rest of the crew, Kiki ran behind the backdrop and searched around. She found the cat huddled in a dusty corner, licking the spot where Kyle had kicked it. "Good kitty," she murmured, taking it in her arms and petting its fuzzy head. "Did you know you look just like my kitten at home?"

On the other side of the backdrop, Kiki could hear Kyle and Marty talking, but she could make out only a few words. "Leading ladies . . . temperamental . . . that stupid cat . . ."

Boy, Kiki thought with dismay, I never thought Kyle would be the type to kick a poor, harmless animal. He always seemed so kind, so considerate. Well maybe he's just tired, she reasoned. We've been working extra hard to finish this film on time, so it's only natural he'd lose his temper once in a while.

Kiki scratched the cat behind its ear and thought about Steve. He would never hurt an animal, no matter how exasperated he was. In fact, as a vet he was going to devote his whole life to healing hurt ones. She thought back to the Christmas morning when he'd arrived at her house with Oz in his arms. Back then Kiki had felt certain she would love Steve forever. Now, picturing his smiling face in her mind, she felt

148

just miserable. Steve's a really special guy, she thought. Why did things have to end so badly?

As Kiki gave the cat's head a pat, Marty stuck his head around the backdrop. "Aileen," he pleaded, "please come out here. We've gotta finish this scene before lunch. We're closing the set down this afternoon."

"Closing the set down?" Kiki asked. Still holding the calico, she walked out from behind the scenery.

"This is Kyle's big day," Marty said. "He's putting his handprints on the sidewalk in front of Grauman's Chinese Theatre. Every reporter in Hollywood will be there."

Kyle walked over to Kiki. "I hope you'll be there, too," he said in a husky voice.

With an angry frown, Kiki looked up at him. He reached out to give the cat in her arms a conciliatory scratch behind the ear. "Sorry, kitty," he said with a regretful smile. "I should have been nicer to you. Any friend of Aileen's is a friend of mine."

Looking at the apologetic expression on Kyle's face, Kiki couldn't help but forgive him. "Of course I'll be there this afternoon," she said warmly. "I wouldn't miss it for the world."

But a sour taste remained in Kiki's mouth. Sure, Kyle was handsome and exciting. And being with him made her feel so special. But she had been seeing a few disturbing things about him lately, too. She couldn't just pretend everything was perfect the way it had been in the beginning.

She petted the cat one last time, then handed

it to the production assistant with instructions to treat it kindly. She went back to the set and took her place with Kyle under the tree. This time, the scene was going to feel more like work than a dream come true.

Chapter Thirteen

"WHAT'S WRONG? YOU DON'T SEEM VERY excited," Kyle said as the studio's chauffeured limo swept them off to Grauman's Chinese Theatre. "This happens to be the biggest moment of my life!"

As he peered at Kiki, she thought she saw a flicker of annoyance in his eyes. No, she told herself. I must be imagining it. Kyle's only concerned about me.

"I'm just tired, Kyle," she replied. "That's all." And no wonder, she thought wearily. I'm living two complete lives in the same amount of time most people live one. Back in Westdale there's school, and homework, and *The Pirates of Penzance* rehearsals. And when I'm in 1939 it's even worse. I'm at the studio from six A.M. until dinnertime or later. I drive home with Doris, and then half an hour later it's time for my date with Kyle. And when I finally get home, I've still got lines to memorize. I don't know how much longer I can keep this up.

But what's the alternative? Kiki wondered. Stop my trips into the past? The idea filled her with dread. My life in the present is a total disaster, she thought miserably. How can I give up being a movie star to return full-time to *that*?

The worst thing of all was that Ashley was threatening not to let Kiki go back to 1939 after she finished making *Stars in Her Eyes*. She'd said Kiki was getting too attached to her life in Hollywood. If she didn't get her head firmly back in the 1980s, Ashley was going to erase the year 1939 completely from Merlin's memory banks, effectively jamming anyone from going there ever again.

Kiki stared blankly out the limo window. They rounded a corner and suddenly her unhappy thoughts were shattered by the roar of the crowd gathered in front of Grauman's Theatre and spilling out into the street.

"Just look at all of them," Kyle said. "We're going to be mobbed by fans and autograph seekers." He groaned, but Kiki noticed an excited glimmer in his eyes.

As the limo pulled to a stop, the people pressed forward, each trying to be the first to get a glimpse of Kyle Kirby. A few women were practically clawing their way to the front of the crowd. One little girl was pushed so hard she fell down on her hands and knees and burst into tears.

Kiki swallowed uncomfortably. Up until now her only public appearances had been at exclusive Hollywood nightclubs where she and Kyle had gone dancing. But this was different, and it made Kiki very nervous. The crowds at the Brown Derby and the Coconut Grove had been polite and well behaved. These people looked like they'd practically kill each other just to get a glimpse of a Hollywood movie star.

But Kyle didn't seem the least bit worried. He pulled a mirror out of his pocket and calmly combed his hair and straightened his tie. Finally, when he looked absolutely perfect, he told the chauffeur to come around and open the door.

Oh well, Kiki reminded herself, trying to get a handle on her rapidly growing fear, the crowd is only here to see Kyle anyway. They probably won't even notice me.

Feeling a little more confident, she stepped out of the limo. The moment her foot touched the curb someone shouted, ''Look, it's Aileen Adair!'' Instantly, the crowd strained forward.

''Miss Adair! Miss Adair! Can I have your autograph?'' a voice cried.

''How does it feel being Kyle Kirby's costar?''

''Hey, Aileen! When's *Stars in Her Eyes* coming out?''

By the time Kyle had joined Kiki on the street, they were completely surrounded by adoring fans. Flashbulbs popped, and reporters shouted question after question. Policemen stepped in to hold back the crowd, pushing overeager stargazers back into the mass of people when they got out of hand.

Kiki tried to look like she was enjoying herself, but it wasn't easy. The intense afternoon sun beating down on her head was even hotter than the movie lights on the set had been. Beads of sweat slid down her forehead. The popping flashbulbs left her blinking against spots which swam before her eyes.

Kiki clutched Kyle's arm and glanced over at him for moral support. But Kyle was off in a world of his own. Flashing his million-dollar smile, he strolled through the crowd like a king among his subjects. Now and then he stopped to sign an autograph or to give a swooning female fan a peck on the cheek. It seemed to take hours to move just a few feet.

When they finally reached the entrance to the theatre, Sid Grauman stepped forward to shake Kyle's hand. While workers poured the cement, Kiki looked around at the other famous handprints and footprints that had been immortalized in the sidewalk. Shirley Temple, Jimmy Stewart, Marlene Dietrich—they were all there, along with dozens of others. Now Kyle would join them. No wonder the crowd was so thrilled. Kiki was beginning to feel that way herself. And, she thought, her excitement growing, someday, if I'm really lucky, maybe I'll be invited to leave my handprints here, too . . .

When the workers finished smoothing the surface of the wet cement, Kyle knelt down with his hands poised over it. Kiki stood beside him, feeling proud to be at the event. She shaded her eyes from the sun and looked around. Reporters and fans pressed forward, all hoping for a glimpse of the historic moment.

Then, suddenly, out of nowhere, a woman in a floppy red hat lunged forward, frantically waving an autograph book. She shoved past Kiki, trying desperately to get to Kyle. As the woman pushed her, Kiki fell sideways—and directly into Kyle.

"Hey!" he yelped, frantically waving his arms to keep his balance. But it was no use. As Kiki watched helplessly, Kyle toppled forward and landed facedown in the wet cement!

Gasping for air, Kyle struggled to his hands and knees. Every inch of his face, his hair, and his suit front were covered with wet, gooey cement. The crowd burst out laughing, and the reporters' flashbulbs popped like machine guns.

"Oh, Kyle," Kiki cried, reaching out to help him. But when he looked up at her, the expression on his face was so black it made her cringe.

Quickly, Kyle turned back to the crowd and quipped, "I've heard of throwing yourself into your work, but this is ridiculous!"

Everyone laughed with delight, and the reporters rushed to write down Kyle's witty line. But Kiki didn't know what to think. Does Kyle blame me for what happened? she wondered anxiously. Can't he see it was that woman's fault?

Kyle wiped his face with his handkerchief and gallantly held out his hand to Kiki. Flashing her a dazzling smile, he said, "Never a dull moment in Tinsel Town, eh, Miss Adair?"

"No, I guess not," she murmured, gazing uncertainly into his face. His smile certainly seemed sincere. Had she just imagined that black look a moment ago? Looking at him now, she wasn't sure.

Kiki frowned. Feeling confused, she took her

place at Kyle's side and watched as the workers poured a fresh load of cement. I guess I'm not sure about much of anything anymore, she thought unhappily. Do I want to stay in the past and go out with Kyle? Do I want to be in Hollywood at all—either past or present? Maybe I should return to present-day Westdale and try to win back Steve's love. And then what? Apply to college? Pursue an acting career there?

Kiki shook her head, as if trying to knock all the elements of her two lives into place. But her world was like a jigsaw puzzle with too many pieces—she just couldn't seem to make them all fit into one picture.

"Okay," Marty called, "this is scene forty-four, take three. Lights, camera . . . action!"

"But Jack"—Kiki stared into Kyle's eyes and recited her line—"you're pure Hollywood. You'd never be happy living in Ohio with me."

Kyle grabbed her shoulders and pulled her close. His mouth was smiling, but his eyes were cold, and Kiki remembered the black look he'd given her the day before outside Grauman's Chinese Theatre. "Try to get it through that beautiful skull of yours," he said. "I'd be happy living anywhere with you. I love you. Besides, where do you think I grew up—on the Sunset Strip? Maybe I never told you this, but I was raised on a farm in Indiana. I'm coming with you, darling, back to Ohio where we both belong."

"Oh, Jack," Kiki murmured, "do you really mean it?"

"Just watch." Kyle pulled her close and kissed her. As their lips touched, Kiki's worries seemed to disappear. She *believed* in that kiss, and it made all her doubts and fears dissolve. The only important thing in the world was the warmth of Kyle's lips and the feel of his arms around her.

"Cut!" Marty shouted enthusiastically. "That's a wrap! And I don't just mean the scene—I mean the whole darn picture!"

Kyle pulled away instantly and turned from Kiki without so much as a "Congratulations on a picture well done." The crew let out a cheer, and Kyle joined in. But Kiki just stood there, unable even to smile. *The way Kyle kissed me,* she thought, *I was sure he really meant it. But as soon as Marty yelled "Cut," he leapt away from me. Why, he's still mad about yesterday, and it wasn't even my fault!*

"Hey, everybody," Marty was saying, "Kyle and I are throwing a big party tonight to celebrate Hollywood's next blockbuster hit—*Stars in Her Eyes.* Eight o'clock at Kyle's place. All the big wheels from around MGM will be there." He grinned broadly. "This movie's gonna be a smash, or my name isn't Marty Lester!"

While the crew started breaking down the set, Marty beckoned Kiki over to him. "At the party tonight," he instructed her, "make sure you and Kyle act real lovey-dovey. Every reporter in Hollywood will be there, and we gotta give them some good photos for the papers tomorrow. The more publicity we can squeeze out of them, the better *Stars in Her Eyes* will do at the box office."

Kiki stared at Marty. Anger, hurt, and disbelief mixed inside her—a crazy kaleidoscope of emotion. Was that why Marty thought she and Kyle had been spending time together? As a publicity stunt? But then an even more horrifying thought occurred to her. Did Kyle feel that way, too? Was his love for her all an act put on for the benefit of the gossip columnists and newspaper photographers?

No, Kiki refused to believe it. She knew a good sincere kiss when she felt one. If Kyle had been faking all along, she would have been able to tell when he held her. So what if he was a little annoyed with her about what had happened at Grauman's Chinese Theatre. It was only a misunderstanding. Hadn't she also been angry at him when he'd lost his temper at the little calico?

Now that they were done with the hard shooting schedule, they wouldn't be so tired and frazzled. Everything would go back to normal. They'd be in love again, passionately, completely, the way they had been at the beginning. They'd be together . . . *if* she could get Ashley to keep sending her into the past.

"You did a good job, kid," Marty said, laying a satisfied hand on Kiki's back. "I'll see you tonight at the party, okay?"

Kiki nodded. "Oh, Marty," she asked, "is it okay if I bring my friend Doris McDougal tonight?"

"Doris McDougal? Who's she?"

"She's a production assistant on *The Wizard of*

158

Oz. I'm staying at her bungalow over on Washington Boulevard.''

Marty winced. ''Washington Boulevard? That's no place for an up-and-coming movie star to live. What if a reporter snapped a picture of you coming out of your apartment one morning? Next thing you know, it would be plastered all over the gossip columns. It would look terrible.'' He shook his head. ''I'll talk to the publicity office. I'm sure they can find you something nice over in Beverly Hills.''

''But about Doris . . .'' Kiki repeated.

''I don't know, Aileen. This Doris McDougal is a nobody. Now that your first movie's coming out, you don't need to hang around with people like her anymore. Besides, I figured you'd be coming with Kyle.''

Kiki glared at Marty, feeling both stunned and furious. How could he be so callous? ''Doris is my friend,'' she said indignantly. ''She helped me when I didn't have any place to go or anybody I could turn to. Why, if it weren't for her, I'd probably be wandering around Hollywood without a dime in my pocket.''

''Hey, relax, Aileen,'' Marty laughed. ''If it means that much to you, bring her along. Just remember, this is a real important night—for both of us. This afternoon I'm going to show some of the unedited film from *Stars in Her Eyes* to Louie Mayer.''

''Who's Louie Mayer?'' Kiki asked.

Marty stared at her. ''Are you kidding me? What do you think MGM stand for? Metro-

159

Goldwyn-*Mayer*, that's what. Louis B. Mayer is the head of the entire MGM studios!''

"Wow!" gasped Kiki. "He's going to see our movie?''

"That's right," Marty replied. "And if he likes it, I'm going to direct his next box-office smash!'' He threw his arm around Kiki's shoulder and gave her a squeeze. "So play your cards right, kid, and you just might end up starring in it . . .''

Chapter Fourteen

"IT MUST FEEL GREAT TO FINISH THE movie," Doris said to Kiki as she drove the Packard up the winding streets of Beverly Hills toward Kyle's house. "We're almost done with *The Wizard of Oz,* too. Just a few short scenes to do tomorrow. We're having a wrap party at Judy Garland's house when it's all over."

"Wow!" exclaimed Kiki. "You mean you're actually going to see the inside of Judy Garland's house?"

Doris laughed. "That's what I like about you, kid. Here you are starring in an MGM movie, and you're still impressed by the thought of going into a movie star's house. Don't you realize *you're* a movie star now, too?

"I just hope *The Wizard of Oz* does okay at the box office," she went on. "MGM has put a lot of money into the film, but I don't know. It seems a little too kooky to be really successful."

"Oh, it'll be successful all right," Kiki said without thinking. "They still show it on TV every single year."

"TV? Oh, you mean that radio station in Connecticut you told me about? But how can they play the music from *The Wizard of Oz* on the radio? The film hasn't even been released to the movie theaters yet."

Kiki blushed right down to the roots of her bleached-blond hair. "Well, I, uh . . ." she stammered. "I mean, I'll bet they *will* play it. That is . . . Oh, never mind. I've just got a hunch it's going to be a big hit."

Doris laughed. "Sounds like a great hunch to me. I hope you're right."

Doris maneuvered the Packard down Beverly Hills Drive and turned into Kyle's curving driveway. It was lined with limos and other fancy cars. A row of tall, pungent eucalyptus trees stood guard at the front of the rambling mansion. "Oh, my gosh!" Doris exclaimed.

Kiki was speechless. Kyle's Spanish-style palace seemed almost as big as O. Henry High School. Ashley's house was like a beach cabin compared to Kyle's place! Every window was blazing with festive lights, and music drifted out of the sweeping, landscaped lawn.

Kiki and Doris stepped out of the car and onto the porch, leaving the Packard to the valets. The doorman opened the front door, bowing slightly, and motioned them through. They walked into the spacious foyer and gazed across the crowded living room. Silk dresses, tails and top hats—everyone looked so glamorous, sipping champagne or dancing to the swing music of the live band.

Kiki let the hem of her own strapless silver evening gown swish luxuriously around her ankles as she worked her way across the room.

What a party of celebrities it was! Lucille Ball was standing by the stairs, sipping a tall drink and laughing at something Leslie Howard was saying. Gosh, thought Kiki, her hair is even redder than I thought. And as Kiki stared wide-eyed, Spencer Tracy handed Katharine Hepburn a drink and gave her a quick kiss on the cheek.

Even hard-boiled Doris was impressed. "Oh, look," she squealed, "there's Humphrey Bogart!" Then she caught herself and added, "He looks a bit older than he does in his movies, don't you think?"

Standing in Kyle's spectacular home surrounded by the greatest stars in the history of Hollywood, Kiki practically felt like fainting from excitement and happiness. But don't you dare faint, she scolded herself, or you might miss a few seconds of the most incredible night of your life!

It was just too marvelous! In less than two weeks, all her wildest dreams had come true. She was a movie star, living in one of the most glamorous decades in the history of Hollywood. Her first movie was about to be released. And, she added, gazing dreamily across the room at Kyle, my leading man is the most handsome man in motion-picture history.

But at the same time, an uneasy feeling tugged at the back of Kiki's mind. This wasn't her life—not really. She was just a teenager, a high-school student from Westdale, Connecticut. And later tonight, when her forty-eight hours were up,

she'd have to go back there—maybe forever—
unless she could convince Ashley to let her keep
coming back.

How can I be happy in modern-day Westdale
after all this? she wondered, gazing across the
room at the twinkling chandeliers, the butlers
with their trays of cocktails and hors d'oeuvres,
and the dozens of famous celebrities. Back home
my parents are mad at me, the kids in school
think I'm a snob, and Steve doesn't love me . . .

"Ah, it's my friend from the Brown Derby ladies' room! Congratulations on the wrap of your
first film."

Kiki looked up to find Joan Crawford smiling
at her. Hey, she reminded herself quickly, this is
no time to be moping about your problems back
home, not while all these famous people are
standing right here in the same room with you.

"Thank you so much, Miss Crawford," Kiki
said eagerly. "I only hope I can develop into
half as good an actress as you are."

Joan Crawford beamed. "How sweet of you to
say so," she replied, taking Kiki's hand and patting it. "But Kyle tells me you're a superbly talented young lady. I'm sure you'll have no trouble
making a name for yourself in show business."

Wow! Kiki thought ecstatically, what a nice
thing for Kyle to say to Joan Crawford! Then he
really does care about me. I *knew* it. Standing
with the star, chatting easily, the moment was
just too perfect for Kiki. She knew she'd savor
it in her heart forever.

"Aileen, can I see you a moment?" It was

Marty, and he looked glum. "Excuse us," he said to Joan Crawford. Taking Kiki's arm, he led her into a corner.

"What's the sad face for, Marty?" Kiki asked. "Everything is so wonderful." She motioned dramatically around the room.

"I showed Louie Mayer the film," Marty said flatly. "He wasn't impressed. Said it was nothing more than a 'B' flick—and not a very good one at that."

"A 'B' flick?" Kiki asked uncertainly. "What do you mean?"

"You know," he answered impatiently. "Grade B. The kind of mediocre movie they show before the big picture, just to get the audience warmed up." He grabbed a cocktail from a passing butler and gulped it down. "The kind of movie I've been making all my life."

Kiki took a closer look at Marty. He looked pale and a little unsteady on his feet. "Are you all right?" she asked with concern.

"No, I am *not* all right," he said in a furious whisper. "I feel lousy." He glared at Kiki. "This was supposed to be my breakthrough picture—the one that was going to put me up there with the big guys. It was a real battle getting Kyle Kirby to star in it, but I convinced the MGM execs I could deliver a box-office smash. And now—" He clenched his fist. "Darn that Mayer! He wouldn't recognize talent if it walked up and slapped him in the face."

As Marty's words slowly sank in, Kiki's high-flying dreams of movie stardom came crashing down around her. Her first film wasn't going to be a hit. In fact, from the way Marty was talking, there was a good chance it was going to be a total bomb.

Kiki wanted to cry, but at the same time, she felt even worse for Marty. He looked so miserable, slouching in the corner with that bitter look on his face. "I'm sorry things didn't work out, Marty," she said, reaching out to touch his shoulder. "But it's not the end of the world. You'll have other chances to prove yourself—I'm sure of it."

Marty just pushed her hand away and muttered, "I never should have gambled on an unknown. It would have taken a real star like Collette to pull this film off. A kid like you just doesn't have what it takes."

Kiki was stunned. Marty was blaming *her* because the picture was a flop. But what did I do wrong? she asked herself. I tried everything I knew about acting to bring that silly script to life. And I went along with each choice Marty made—even dyeing my hair blond and talking in that silly, high, breathy voice. "But Marty," she began, "how did I—?"

"Forget it, kid," he said irritably. "Just forget it." He ran his hand over his face and muttered, "I gotta get some fresh air." Before Kiki could say another word, he pushed past her and disappeared into the crowd.

Standing alone in the corner, Kiki gazed blankly down at the floor and tried to make sense of things. Maybe it *is* my fault the film isn't any good, she thought. Marty's made dozens of films before, so he must know what he's talking about. I'm just an amateur, a nobody. I don't have what it takes. She looked desperately around the room for a comforting face. No one. Except . . .

Doris was walking across the room toward her, grinning from ear to ear. "Kiki, you'll never guess who I just met! Humphrey Bogart and— Hey, you look like the world just fell apart on you."

"It has," Kiki moaned. Tearfully, she told Doris everything Marty had just said. "A couple of weeks ago Marty promised to make me a star," she finished unhappily. "Now he's treating me like I'm that little cat who wandered onto the set by mistake. What happened?"

Doris wrapped a comforting arm around her friend's shoulder. "Poor Kiki," she sympathized. "I tried to warn you—that's how it goes in Hollywood. They don't call it Tinsel Town for nothing."

Kiki fought back sobs. She *couldn't* cry, not right here in front of everybody. "Is it really my fault Mr. Mayer didn't like the film?" she asked. "I didn't think I was all *that* bad."

"I'm sure you did a good job," Doris said firmly. "I heard you practicing your lines, and I know you really put your whole self into the part. Marty just doesn't want to admit it might be *his* fault that the film's a failure, so he blamed you instead."

Kiki's lower lip trembled. "Five minutes ago, Joan Crawford was telling me I had a great career ahead of me, and now I feel like a total has-been.''

Doris gave Kiki's shoulders a gentle squeeze. ''Hey, I'm sorry, kid,'' she said softly. ''But your head was so full of dreams that you couldn't see what Hollywood is really like. In this business, it's all smiles and kisses . . . but only as long as you're on top.''

So that's the way it is, Kiki thought miserably. All the flattery, the limo rides, and red carpets—none of it means a thing. ''But what about Kyle?'' she asked, her eyes filling with tears. ''He's not like the others. He really cares about me—I know he does.''

But Doris just smiled sadly. Kiki felt a surge of anger sweep through her. *What does Doris know? She thinks Kyle is just like everyone else. But he's not. He doesn't care if I'm a big Hollywood movie star or a plain old high-school student from Westdale, Connecticut. He loves me for myself.*

Suddenly, Kiki had to find Kyle. She needed his strong arms around her, his lips against hers. Having him near would make her believe that she was still the brightest star in the galaxy. Turning her back on Doris, she hurried through the crowd, looking for his handsome face.

Kiki searched the living room, the foyer, even the kitchen, but Kyle was nowhere to be found. Making her way up the curving marble staircase to the second floor, she headed for the expansive marble balcony overlooking the living room. She could see people dancing, smiling, laughing. And as she neared the landing, she spotted

168

Kyle. He was standing in the corner, snapping his fingers in time to the swing music which wafted gently up from the main room.

Kiki bounded up the last few stairs. But as she started across the balcony, she saw that Kyle wasn't alone. With him was a glamorous blond in a daring, low-cut gown and a flashy diamond tiara. And when Kiki realized who it was, she thought her heart was going to stop. Collette. As Kiki watched, horrified, the starlet stood on her tiptoes and kissed Kyle full on the lips!

Kiki could barely believe her eyes. What's *she* doing here? she wondered with dismay. Then everything fell into place. Collette's heard that Mr. Mayer doesn't like the picture, so she's come back to gloat. But Kyle won't be taken in by her. Any minute now, he'll tell her to get lost. With a confident smile, Kiki hid behind a potted palm and waited to see what would happen.

"Well, the divorce is official," Collette said, running her scarlet fingernails seductively across Kyle's cheek. "I'm a single woman again. Single . . . and available."

Kiki was fuming. It was all she could do to keep from stepping out from behind the plant and slapping Collette in the face. But she kept her calm. Leaning closer, she waited for Kyle's reply.

"You know, Collette," he said, "between you and me, I'm glad *Stars in Her Eyes* is finished. Aileen is a no-talent nobody. A hick from the sticks. Now, if *you* had been my costar, I'm sure things would have been different." He took her hand and added, "I'd rather do just one scene with you than a thousand movies with Aileen Adair.'' Flashing Collette the same sexy smile Kiki had been seeing for the last two weeks, he lifted her hand to his lips and kissed it.

Kiki felt like someone had dumped a bucket of ice water over her head. She'd believed Kyle loved her. Tears flooded her eyes, and she ached as if she'd been punched.

Collette's tinkling laughter drifted across the balcony. ''But Kyle,'' she cooed, ''you two are the hottest item in all the gossip columns these days. I've seen the articles—dinner at the Brown Derby, dancing at the Coconut Grove, and passionate love scenes on the set all day long.''

Kyle laughed. ''Oh, come on, Collette. You should know better than to believe those fan magazines. It was all a gimmick, a publicity ploy.''

''That's not what Hedda Hopper told me,'' Collette said with a coy pout.

Kyle frowned. ''Forget what you heard. The front office cooked the whole thing up to help sell the picture. But Marty's gotten the word from the studio heads that the movie's going to bomb, thanks to Miss Hayseed. And let's just say that when the ship sinks, I don't want to be on it.''

Kiki couldn't bear to listen anymore. Now she knew what heartache really meant. Her whole chest was throbbing with a dull, empty pain. ''Kyle doesn't love me,'' she whispered. The words stung. Unable to hold the bitter tears back another moment, she dashed down the stairs and pushed her way through the crowd, not even noticing which famous star she was passing.

"Why, Aileen," someone called cheerily, "where are you off to in such a hurry?"

"Oh, Miss Adair," another voice called, "don't go. We're just dying to hear all about your new movie!"

But Kiki couldn't answer. Suddenly, all the glitter and glamour, the smiles and compliments, seemed unbearably cheap and phony. She wanted to go home right away!

Home! She pictured the town green covered with a blanket of clean, white snow. The family deli, all warm and cozy and filled with the delicious smells of fresh bread and pickles and pastrami. And O. Henry High, with its familiar ivy-draped walls and the simple, romantic, old wishing well behind it. If only she could be there right now, hugging Steve close to her.

Oh, Steve, Kiki thought sadly, where are you now? She pictured his handsome face and his warm, easy, sincere smile, and the tears spilled onto her cheeks. How could I ever have fallen for a two-faced phony like Kyle when the best boyfriend in the world was right there in my own backyard?

The really important things in life were all back home—like good friends and loving parents and . . . Steve. Because all those people really cared about her. So what if Westdale wasn't the hot spot of the Eastern Seaboard. People had fun there without champagne and swooning fans and big, fake, flattering speeches.

Kiki decided that if she saw one more pasted-on smile, she was going to scream, no matter how many famous stars were in the room. What's happened to real conversations here? Don't people ever have them? Is it all just an act, off camera as well as on? Kiki wiped her tears away with the back of her hand, not caring that she was smearing her eyeliner.

Kiki pushed open a set of French doors and ran outside into the cool evening air. She found herself on a stone patio, overlooking a kidney-shaped swimming pool. What a joke, she thought bitterly. All my life I've dreamed of this—Beverly Hills mansions, palm trees, parties, movie stars. And now that I'm here, I find out it's all a bunch of grade-B baloney. The whole thing's a sham, a fake. Just like Kyle's love.

Staring into the darkness, Kiki felt like the biggest fool who had ever lived. Why hadn't she seen how things really were—both in Hollywood and in Westdale? How could she have been taken in by the rhinestone dazzle of a place like Beverly Hills?

It was her own fault that her life in the present was such a mess. She'd hurt her parents, alienated her friends, and driven away her boyfriend—all for the sake of a few moments of Hollywood stardom. And, now, what did she have to show for it? Just a box-office flop and a broken heart. Overwhelmed with unhappiness, Kiki put her head in her hands and burst into tears.

Chapter Fifteen

"NOW THAT'S SOMETHING I HATE TO SEE," came a voice from a dark corner of the patio. "What's a girl like you doing sitting out here all alone, crying her heart out?"

With a surprised gasp, Kiki lifted her head from her hands and stared dimly in the direction of the voice. A heavyset man was sitting on a stone bench near the pool, smoking a fat cigar. Quickly, Kiki wiped the tears from her eyes and forced herself to smile. She might be miserable, but she had too much pride to let some stranger catch her crying. Taking a deep breath, she stepped forward and said in what she hoped was a cheery voice, "I just came out for a breath of air."

"Same here," the man said in a gravelly voice. "I hate these Hollywood parties, don't you? Just a lot of stars massaging their egos, if you ask me."

Despite her unhappiness, Kiki had to laugh. She walked a little closer to get a better look at the man on the bench. He was middle-aged, with gray hair, a large nose, and dark-rimmed

173

glasses. "You're right," she said. "But if you feel that way about it, why did you come in the first place?"

"Wouldn't look right if I didn't. Head of the studio and all—you know how it is. Besides, that's what Hollywood's all about. Celebrities . . . parties . . . publicity. It comes with the territory." He shrugged and took a puff on his cigar.

Head of the studio? With a start, Kiki realized who she was talking to. It was none other than Louis B. Mayer, the owner of MGM Studios and the man who had panned *Stars in Her Eyes*! "Oh, Mr. Mayer," she blurted out, blushing with embarrassment, "Marty Lester told me you didn't like our movie, and I'm really sorry. I know I wasn't very good, but, well, it was my first film, and, uh—"

"It's true," Louis B. Mayer said frankly. "I thought the film was a dog."

"Uh, yes, sir. And to tell you the truth, I've never acted in anything except high-school plays before this. So . . ." Her voice trailed off, and she finished in a whisper. "I guess I'm just not cut out to be a movie star."

But to Kiki's surprise, Mr. Mayer grinned at her, waving aside her apology with the glowing tip of his cigar. "Just because I didn't like the picture doesn't mean I didn't like you. Matter of fact, you were the best thing about it."

"Really?" Kiki gasped, hardly daring to believe what she was hearing. "You mean, I did okay?"

174

"Better than okay. Much better. Let me tell you, young lady, you've got what it takes. All you need is a little more experience. Now listen here"—he jabbed his cigar for emphasis— "MGM is testing actresses right now for a part in a very important new project. I want you at the studio tomorrow morning for a screen test. It wouldn't be the lead, mind you, but you wouldn't be throwing your pearls before a swine like Marty Lester, either. And after that, well, who knows? You've got the looks and the talent to go all the way—if you keep working hard."

Kiki was stunned. How incredible! Louis B. Mayer is practically guaranteeing me a part in his next movie! Any struggling actress would sell her smile for a chance like this. All I have to do is keep coming back to 1939, and I'll *really* be a Hollywood movie star in no time!

But something was keeping Kiki from jumping at the offer. It was a great opportunity, sure, but was it what she really wanted? A few hours ago she would have said yes. But that was when she'd still thought Hollywood was a perfect world, populated only by beautiful people. Now she knew the truth. Beneath all the glamour and glitz, there was nastiness and backstabbing, and plenty of self-centered phonies like Kyle, Marty, and Collette.

After everything she'd been through, the idea of auditioning for another MGM movie just didn't seem all that appealing. What I really want to do is act, she told herself, not spend my time worrying about Hollywood politics and gossip. And the best place to start is back in Westdale, in the O. Henry High production of *The Pirates of Penzance*. Come to think of it, even filling out those college applications doesn't sound all that bad anymore. Some of those schools have excellent drama departments. I just might learn a few things that will really help me with my acting career.

"Thanks Mr. Mayer," Kiki said, "but I can't audition for your new movie. I'm going home to Connecticut. I have a friend who's really talented, though. Her name's Doris McDougal." Kiki smiled to herself. Not everyone in Hollywood is a phony. Doris has helped me out more than all the other people I've met here combined . . .

"I'd really appreciate it if you let her audition for that part instead of me," Kiki continued. "I know you won't be sorry."

"Well," Mr. Mayer said gruffly, "if she's half as good as you, then I won't be wasting my time."

Kiki grinned. "Believe me, you won't, Mr. Mayer. Now if you'll excuse me, there's one last thing I have to do before I head home."

Leaving Mr. Mayer puffing pensively on his cigar, Kiki hurried back inside and called over one of the white-jacketed waiters. "I have an important message for Mr. Kirby," she told him. She took a fountain pen Doris had lent her from her evening bag and scribbled a note on a cocktail napkin. "Great news! Meet me at the pool right away—Aileen." Kiki handed the napkin to the butler. "Tell him it's urgent," she said.

The waiter took off toward the balcony and Kiki strolled back out to the patio. Mr. Mayer was gone—to look for Doris, she hoped—and there was no one else in sight. The night was cool and clear, and a romantic full moon hung over the Hollywood Hills. But despite the beauty of the evening, Kiki couldn't wait to get home—back to the familiar snow-covered streets of Westdale, back to her friends and her family. Back to Steve.

Oh, how she longed to see him again—to hear his warm laughter and feel her hand in his. Closing her eyes, she imagined his clear green eyes, his wavy blond hair, and his soft flannel shirts. No, he didn't belong here in glittery, glamour Hollywood. He'd stick out like a sore thumb at a party like this one. But now, instead of being disappointed at the thought, Kiki was glad! Steve would take one look around here and know the place was filled with phonies. Nope, Steve just wasn't the Hollywood type. He was much too down-to-earth, much too *real*.

With a sharp pang, Kiki recalled the night they'd decided to "cool it" for a while. Had Steve made up his mind to break up with her permanently? Was it too late for a second chance? She hoped with all her heart it wasn't.

Kiki felt a warm hand on her arm. Turning, she found Kyle beside her. "I got your note, but I would have come anyway," he said, flashing his million-dollar smile. "I saw you from the upstairs window talking to Mayer. I've never seen him grin that way at anyone! So he must have liked the picture after all, huh?''

Kyle moved closer and put his arm around Kiki's shoulders. The touch that had once thrilled her now felt unbearably clammy, and the pressure of Kyle's palm against her bare skin made her squirm. But she forced herself to smile sweetly and say, ''Come on, Kyle, let's walk down by the pool.''

Together they made their way across the patio and down the stone steps that led to the kidney-shaped swimming pool.

''I saw you talking to Collette,'' Kiki said casually.

For an instant, Kyle's smile faltered. But then he turned to Kiki and slipped both arms around her waist. ''Yes, I couldn't help it. She practically backed me into a corner.'' He shook his head disdainfully. ''Can you believe the nerve of that woman? First she walks off the picture to divorce her fourth husband, and now she shows up at the wrap party. I guess she heard Mr. Mayer likes the film and she's hoping to get in on the action.''

I could say the same thing about you, Kyle dear, Kiki thought in disgust. But she kept her feelings to herself. She smiled and looked past Kyle's shoulder at the gentle ripples on the surface of the swimming pool behind him. ''Mr. Mayer wants me to act in his next picture,'' she told him. ''He said I have the looks and the talent to go all the way.''

Kyle responded by tilting Kiki's chin toward him until their lips were only inches apart. "I'm not at all surprised. From the first moment I set eyes on you," he whispered in a soft, seductive voice, "I knew you were something special."

"Is that right?" Kiki replied. "Well, you know, I told Mr. Mayer he ought to consider using you in the film, too. There's a part that sounds as if it's perfect for you . . ."

Kyle's eyes lit up and he leaned forward eagerly to kiss her. But just as their lips were about to touch, Kiki slammed her hands against his chest and gave him a firm shove.

". . . as a snake!" she finished with a satisfied nod.

Arms flailing, Kyle fell backward—and right into the pool. With a loud splash, he hit the water and disappeared beneath the surface. A second later he shot up, sputtering and gasping for air. His dark hair was plastered over his forehead and his starched tuxedo collar hung limply around his neck. "Why, you . . . you . . . !" he blubbered.

Kiki took one look at the outraged expression on his face and burst out laughing. Kyle Kirby wasn't so suave and dashing now. His handsome face twisted with rage, he was finally showing his true colors.

"How dare you laugh at me, you ungrateful little wretch!" Kyle shouted. Paddling furiously, he worked his way toward the edge of the pool. "I'll get you for this!" he gasped. "You'll never work in Hollywood again! Why, when I get through with you, you'll be *begging* for work!''

''Big deal,'' Kiki giggled. ''I've got better things to do.'' Already, her fingers and toes were tingling. Glancing down at her legs, she saw that she was beginning to evaporate.

Kyle dragged himself out of the pool and stared at her. ''What's going on?'' His eyes grew as wide as saucers. ''Good gravy,'' he cried, his voice trembling, ''you're disappearing!''

Kiki thought of ducking out of sight, but then she changed her mind. Let *him* figure out what happened, she decided with satisfaction. ''So long, Kyle,'' she called. ''See you in the movies!''

The last thing she saw before she vanished completely was Kyle frantically rubbing his watery eyes with his knuckles. ''It can't be,'' he gasped fearfully. ''I . . . must be losing my mind!''

Then Kiki felt herself falling into the swirl of colors that would bring her back to the present. I feel just like Dorothy at the end of *The Wizard of Oz*, she thought. Smiling, she clicked her heels together and repeated the magic words just the way Judy Garland had: ''There's no place like home . . . there's no place like home . . .''

Chapter Sixteen

"KIKI, WHERE HAVE YOU BEEN?" MAMA asked as Kiki threw off her coat and joined the family at the dining-room table. "When you ran out of the house so upset a little while ago, we were worried."

"I'm sorry, Mama," Kiki answered. "I was over at Ashley's house." Looking around the cozy kitchen, Kiki couldn't help but smile. The linoleum was still worn in spots, and the red-checked curtains around the window that over-looked the parking lot were as faded as ever. There was the old brown cookie jar on the counter, cracked from the time Mama had caught her sneaking cookies before dinner and Kiki had pulled her hand out so fast she'd knocked it over. Tears of happiness filled her eyes. Maybe it wasn't exactly the Brown Derby, but right now it seemed like the most wonderful place on earth. She reached toward the large casserole dish and lifted the lid, releasing a cloud of delicious-smelling steam. "Stuffed cabbage!" she exclaimed. "Just what I was hoping for!"

"You certainly have been spending a lot of

time at Ashley's house lately," Papa said. He looked tired, his eyes rimmed with red, as he sat hunched over his plate, still wearing his deli apron. "Is she also planning to skip college and become an actress?"

"Ashley?" Kiki said, helping herself to a mound of cabbage. "No way! She's a computer-whiz. She'll probably be teaching at MIT before she's twenty-one. But Papa, listen, I have something important I want to talk to you about."

"Yes? Well, fine, but let me say a few words first." He straightened and cleared his throat, his expression solemn. "Kiki, I want to apologize. For years you've been telling me you want to be an actress, but I listened with only half an ear." He leaned forward, a pleading look on his face. "You see, in Poland, I didn't have any time for things like acting, or music, or art. My family were simple shopkeepers, and it took all our energy just to make enough money to stay alive."

"But Papa, I—"

Mr. Wykowski held up his hand for silence. "Let me finish. I came to America because I wanted my children to have all the things I never had. I wanted them to grow up in a country where they could get an education and a good job. But to me, a good job meant working in an office or a hospital or a classroom—it meant being a doctor, or a lawyer, or a teacher, or a nurse. It never occurred to me that one of my daughters would want to be an *actress*." He shrugged. "But now that I'm finally getting used to the idea, I figure why shouldn't my Kiki

be an actress? In America, *anything* is possible."
He looked at Kiki and smiled warmly. "Isn't
that right, my New-World daughter?"

"What Papa means to say," Mama broke in,
"is that if you want to make acting your career,
it's all right with us." In her old flowered dress,
her dark hair streaked with gray, and her hands
red and chapped, she was the most beautiful
woman in the world to Kiki. More beautiful than
the most glamorous Hollywood star.

"Yes," Papa nodded. "But one more thing. I
went back through those college catalogues again,
and do you know what I found out? You can go
to college and *still* be an actress. There are special
programs in dramatic arts!"

"But, Kiki," Mama finished, "if you decide
that even those acting programs aren't right for
you . . . well, we'll do our best to understand.
And in the end, no matter what you choose to
do with your life, we want you to know you
have our blessing."

Kiki was overwhelmed. A lump formed in her
throat. She knew it wasn't easy for her parents
to accept the fact that she wanted to act. And to
give her their blessing—much more than Kiki
had ever hoped for.

Now, looking at her parents, tears of love and
joy welled up in her eyes. "Mama, Papa," she
said, "you're the best parents in the whole
world." She pushed a blond curl back under her
scarf and took a deep breath. "And now I have
something to tell you. I've been thinking about
my future a lot these past few weeks, and I think

I've finally figured things out. As far as my acting goes, I may have some talent, but I still have a heck of a lot to learn. And that's why I've decided I *do* want to go to college. I'll take acting classes—and lots of other courses besides. And after the first two years, if I decide acting is still what I really want to do, I'll major in dramatic arts."

"Oh, Kiki," Mama cried, "that's wonderful!"

"Maybe later we can look through those catalogues again," Papa said eagerly. He took a bite of cabbage and added, "You know, I noticed Yale has a very good drama department."

Hmm, Kiki mused, Yale. That's where Jennifer Beals went. Sounds pretty good. She munched her stuffed cabbage and slipped into a daydream. She and Jennifer Beals were riding together in a sleek black limousine, on their way to the premiere of their new movie. As they pulled up in front of the theater, Kiki looked up at the marquee:

Kiki Wykowski and Jennifer Beals
In Their New Smash-Hit Movie:
Flashdance II

But Kiki never got to step out of the limo because her little sister interrupted her daydream. "What's for dessert, Mama?" Mimi asked.

"Yeah," complained Jenna, "you three were talking so much, you didn't even notice that Mimi and I cleaned our plates."

Kiki and her parents laughed. "All right, girls," Mama said warmly, "there's a fresh apple pie on the counter in the kitchen. Jenna, why don't you go in and get it? But be careful. I don't want pie on the dining-room rug!''

As Jenna ran to get the dessert, Kiki turned to her mother and asked sheepishly, ''Mama, one more thing. Do you think you could help me dye my hair back to its natural color? And then if we cut it, it would look a little less old-fashioned.''

Mama chuckled happily. ''Kiki, darling, I thought you'd never ask.''

''You know, Oz,'' Kiki said thoughtfully, gazing into the mirror, ''I think I like it.'' Thanks to Mama's skilled attention, her hair was back to its original dark brown color and most of the curls were gone. Kiki worked some mousse into her bangs. ''The question is,'' she said anxiously, ''will Steve like it, too?''

She certainly hoped so. Just thinking about him made her pulse quicken. I miss him so much, she thought longingly. But does he miss me, too? Judging by the way he's been acting lately, the answer is no. But there's only one way to find out. I have to talk to him. And what better time than now?

With her stomach churning, Kiki walked into the kitchen and picked up the phone. Halfway through dialing Steve's number, she remembered the afternoon when she'd run into him outside of history class. He'd behaved as if he could hardly stand to talk to me, she thought sadly. And he's been avoiding me ever since. She frowned. I thought our relationship was on hold. But he acts like it's completely over. Could it be he's found someone else? she wondered. It made sense. Why else would he have dropped her cold?

Suddenly, Kiki felt panic-stricken at the thought of hearing Steve's voice. She couldn't bear to talk to him—not if it meant having him tell her they were through. Quickly she put the receiver back on the hook.

Maybe I'll call Ramona instead, she thought. I need to talk to somebody about what's been happening, and I know she'll understand. She picked up the phone again and dialed, thinking all the while of Steve's handsome profile and his warm, inviting smile.

The phone rang twice. There was a click and then a male voice said, "Hello?"

Kiki's heart froze. She'd know that voice anywhere. "Steve!" she gasped, "what are you doing at Ramona's house?"

"Huh? Kiki, is that you?"

"Um, yes, but, uh—isn't Ramona there?"

"No, of course not. Why would Ramona be at my house?" Without waiting for an answer, he asked, "Didn't you want to talk to me?"

"No," Kiki blurted out. "I mean, yes. Well, not exactly. It's just, uh—"

"I think I understand," he said coldly. "Look, I gotta go. Bye." With that, the line went dead.

Kiki just stood there, staring at the phone and feeling like a complete idiot. What in the world made me dial Steve's number? she asked herself. And then, when I heard his voice, why didn't I just pretend I'd been calling him all along? Why did I have to act like such a fool?

For a fleeting moment, Kiki considered calling Steve back. But the cold, flat sound of his voice saying good-bye echoed through her mind. It's over between us, she thought sadly. If I wasn't sure of it before, I am now. With a heavy heart, she put down the phone and walked away. She couldn't get herself to call Ramona now. She was just too depressed to have a good conversation.

Back in her room, Kiki closed the door and lay down on the bed next to Oz. Tears poured down her cheeks, forming a damp spot on the worn chenille bedspread. "Oh, Oz," she asked sorrowfully, "what good is being back in the present if I can't have Steve?" The kitten replied with a mournful meow.

Out in the hallway, Kiki could hear the phone ringing. "Kiki," Mama called, "it's for you."

A spark of hope flickered in her heart. Maybe it's Steve, she thought. Maybe he's calling back to tell me he still loves me. Wiping the tears from her cheeks, she hurried to the kitchen and picked up the phone. "Hello?"

"Hi! It's me, Tina. Have you decided what you're wearing to the 'Hello, Dolly' dance tomorrow night?"

"Th—the what?"

"The *dance*. I just bought this totally incredible ivory-colored lace with a low-cut neck. Just wait till you see it!"

The "Hello, Dolly" dance! So much had been going on in Kiki's life recently that she'd forgotten all about it. Now, with the dance only a day away, filling out Tina's questionnaire seemed like a terrible mistake. I already *know* how I feel about Steve, she thought sadly. And I don't want to date anyone else, no matter who Ashley's computer matches me up with. "Uh, I don't think I'm going tomorrow night," Kiki said. "I, uh, don't feel very well. I think I might be coming down with something."

"Don't be silly," Tina said firmly. "It's all those trips into the past that are making you feel that way. You need to get back in touch with the present. And there's no better way than to dance the night away with some handsome new boy."

"But I don't want a new boy. I want Steve." Kiki was close to tears. "The only problem is, he doesn't love me anymore. He's in love with someone else."

"I don't believe it," Tina said firmly. "But if he *is* seeing another girl, that's all the more reason to come to the dance. Moping around at home will only make you feel worse."

"Well . . ."

"Please come," Tina said earnestly. "It would really mean a lot to me. I mean, this whole computer-date thing was my idea, and if nobody shows up, I'll feel like a real fool."

After hearing a confession like that, Kiki couldn't very well back out. Besides, she thought, what difference does it make? I'll be equally miserable whether I'm at home or at the dance. "Oh, all right," she said. "I'll be there."

"Terrific!" Tina exclaimed. "And don't forget, Kiki, wear something beautiful and romantic. Tomorrow night is meant for love."

Chapter Seventeen

KIKI FOLLOWED RAMONA AND BOB across the parking lot toward O. Henry High. Thank goodness Ramona offered me a ride, she thought gratefully. Coming to the dance all alone would have been just too awful.

"Looks like a great turn-out," Ramona said, surveying the crowded parking lot.

"Yeah," Bob agreed. "And I'm ready to party!" He grabbed Ramona and broke into a few quick dance steps across the snow-covered lawn.

"Stop it, you nut!" Ramona giggled. "I'm getting snow in my shoes!"

Kiki smiled, but her heart just wasn't in it. She gazed toward the grove of trees which hid O. Henry High's wishing well. The last time she'd been there was the afternoon she and Steve had broken up. If only I could rewind my life like a videocassette, she thought longingly. I'd go back to that night and do it all over again. And this time, when Steve suggested cooling it for a while, I'd throw my arms around him and tell him I loved him with all my heart.

"Hey," Ramona said, "are you okay?" Kiki

shrugged and her friend came over to give her a sympathetic hug. "Just try to relax and have fun tonight," Ramona said. She smiled and added, "In that outfit, you'll probably have every guy in the school after you."

That morning Kiki had gone back to Ashley's house and retrieved the strapless silver evening gown. She'd added a soft, berry-colored shawl and a string of matching glass beads. Her hair swirled naturally around her shoulders, and she'd filled out her 1930s' brows with the help of some brown eyebrow pencil. Not that it really mattered how she looked, though. Who cared if every guy in school was after her. The only one I want is Steve, she thought. And I can't have him. Feeling even more miserable than she had on her last night in 1939, Kiki followed Ramona and Bob into the darkened gym.

Once inside, Kiki had to admit that Tina and J. C. had done a wonderful job decorating the place. The room was aglow with strings of tiny twinkling white lights left over from Christmas. Paper hearts, cupids, and computer cards covered the walls, and bunches of multicolored balloons floated over the doors. In one corner, J. C. was acting as deejay. He was poised over two turntables, carefully controlling the segue from one song to the next.

"Come on, Ramona," Bob said, "let's dance. And Kiki, save the next one for me, okay?" Kiki nodded, but her mind was on other things. Who am I going to get matched up with? she wondered nervously. Nerdy Malcolm Thurston walked by in a suit and tie—and his pants were so short they were practically up to his armpits. Oh please, she prayed, not him. Buck Warren caught her eye and smiled. He was the star fullback on the football team. Gorgeous—but he wasn't Steve Goldman, and as far as Kiki was concerned, that counted him out.

Maybe my date won't even show up, Kiki thought, and I'll have to spend the whole evening standing in the corner by myself. Well, that would probably be better than having to make chitchat with some date I don't even know or care about. Suddenly, the idea of hiding out in the girls' room all night seemed the only sensible solution.

"Why, Kiki, hello!" It was Clarissa Van Dyke, and her eyes were practically popping out of her head as she stared at Kiki's beautiful short hairstyle. "Everyone's talking about your new look. No more scarf and sunglasses, huh?"

Kiki nodded. All day during school kids had been coming up and asking the same question. She told Clarissa exactly what she'd told the others. "Consider them a failed experiment," she said. "From now on, the old Kiki is back."

"And what about your old boyfriend?" Clarissa asked with an unpleasant smile. "Have you got him back, too?"

The words cut like a knife, but Kiki forced herself to ignore the way they made her ache. "Clarissa," she asked sweetly, "I was just wondering. Do you have any relatives in Los Angeles?"

"Uh, no. Why?"

"Oh, nothing. It's just that you remind me of someone I once knew. Louella Parsons—the biggest blabbermouth in all of Hollywood!"

Clarissa looked like she'd just gotten a swift kick in the pants. "Well!" she gasped. "I . . . I . . ."

But before she could get another word out, the music stopped and J. C. McCloskey leaned close to the microphone. "This is it, folks," he quipped. "All you lucky people who filled out questionnaires are about to be matched up with the boy or girl of your dreams. Just step up to the tables over by the bleachers. Our hard working dance committee can't wait to give you the name of your mystery love."

J. C. cued in another record as kids began moving toward the spot where Tina and a few other members of the *Herald* staff were sitting. But Kiki just stood still, wishing she could dig a hole and crawl into it. She watched Ramona and Bob walking toward her, holding hands happily.

"Go on, Kiki," Bob said. "I bet you some great guy is waiting for you over there."

"Well . . ." she muttered reluctantly.

"Oh, Kiki," Ramona exclaimed, "how bad can it be?"

Very bad, Kiki thought. The worst. Still, it was too late to back out now. With a sigh, she walked over with the rest of the crowd. "Okay, Miss Lonelyhearts, hand over my sentence," she said to Tina.

Tina giggled and gave Kiki an envelope which had her name and a red heart on it. "Good luck," she said enthusiastically. "And remember, think romance!"

"Yeah, sure." Feeling miserable and just a little annoyed at Tina for having talked her into filling out a questionnaire in the first place, Kiki stepped away from the table and ripped open the envelope. Inside was a computer card with the name of her date typed across it. "Steve Goldman?" she cried out loud. "I don't believe it!" She stared at the card in amazement. Merlin had matched her and Steve up!

"I didn't believe it at first, either," said a familiar voice behind her. Spinning around, Kiki found herself face-to-face with Steve. He was wearing a black corduroy jacket and skinny knitted tie, and he looked terrific. With her heart pounding, she gazed into his eyes, trying to read the expression on his face. Was he disappointed? Unhappy? Mad?

Steve held up the computer card with her name on it. "My mystery date is the prettiest girl in all of Connecticut," he said softly. He flashed her an uncertain smile and added sheepishly, "I just hope you're not too disappointed with the guy you got matched up with."

That was all Kiki needed to hear. She threw her arms around Steve and cried, "I couldn't be more thrilled if I'd just won an Academy Award! I missed you so much! More than I ever thought I would."

"I missed you, too," he said. "When I heard your voice on the phone last night, I was so happy. But then you asked for Ramona and I figured it was just a mistake. You didn't mean to call me at all."

"I *wanted* to call you," Kiki explained. "I started to, but I chickened out. Then when I tried to call Ramona, I dialed your number instead by accident." She bit her lip. "But I was so nervous that I totally blew the conversation, and when you hung up so fast I decided it proved you didn't care about me anymore."

Steve looked confused. "Are you kidding? I never wanted to break up. It's just that you didn't seem very happy with me. That was why I suggested we cool it for a while. I wanted to give you a chance to back out of the relationship—if that's what you wanted."

Kiki laughed ruefully. "I thought I did. But boy was I wrong." She thought about Kyle Kirby and shook her head. What a fool I was, she told herself. Sure he was a handsome Hollywood movie star. But underneath the good looks and the glamour, he was nothing—a complete zero. She smiled happily at Steve. I went all the way back to 1939 looking for the perfect guy, and it turns out he was right here all the time. "Steve," she said earnestly, "I don't want to be with anyone but you. Past, present, *and* future."

Steve grinned. "I guess it's not so surprising that the computer matched us up. I mean, I always knew we had a lot in common. We both love animals, and old movies . . ."

"Right," Kiki agreed. "And spicy food, and acting in school plays . . ."

"And dancing." With a loving smile, he held

out his arms. "So what are we just standing here for? The music's right and so's my date. Let's dance."

Kiki let out a contented sigh as Steve enfolded her in a tender, loving hug. With her head resting on his shoulder, they danced slowly across the floor, swaying together to the hypnotic beat. The feel of Steve's strong body so close to hers made Kiki's legs feel weak. She closed her eyes and breathed in the fresh smell of his skin and his hair.

Being with Kyle Kirby was never like this, she thought dreamily. He always made me feel nervous and unsure of myself. I couldn't even be Kiki Wykowski around him. I was always Aileen Adair. Kiki knew she'd had some powerful feelings for Kyle, but she'd finally figured out exactly what they were. It hadn't been love. It was infatuation. She'd been impressed with him and she'd wanted him to like her, but that was all there was to it. She snuggled closer to Steve. This, she sighed happily, is love.

"I missed having you close to me like this," Steve whispered in her ear.

"It feels great to be back," Kiki breathed. "And I learned something, too."

"You did?" Steve said gently, reaching up to stroke her hair.

Kiki smiled at him. "I learned that you don't have to go to the end of the rainbow to find a pot of gold. Sometimes it's right there in front of you." She shrugged. "It just took me a while to see it, that's all."

"Mmm," Steve murmured, "I think I see my

pot of gold right now." He leaned down and gave her a long, lingering kiss that sent waves of pleasure down her spine. The slow, romantic song ended and a faster one came on. All around Kiki and Steve, kids were dancing and talking. But as far as Kiki was concerned, she and Steve were all alone, lost in a kiss that was much better than any crazy fantasy she could ever dream up.

Kiki flopped down on her bed and opened *The Complete Encyclopedia of Movies and Movie Stars*. Immediately, Oz padded over and stretched out across the pages.

"Oz," Kiki scolded, "how do you expect me to find Doris in here if you're going to use the book for a pillow? Besides," she added, picking up the kitten and dropping her gently to the floor, "this is a library book. I can't very well return it with cat hair between the pages."

Oz let out a meow and turned her attention to her toy catnip mouse. Smiling, Kiki rested her head on her arm and watched the kitten. It felt great to be back home. The smell of Mama's cooking, the sounds of Jenna and Mimi playing in the next room, the silly look on Oz's face as she batted the toy mouse—it all felt so comfortable, so reassuring, so *right*. I never would have believed it a few days ago, she thought, but I really don't miss anything about Hollywood—except Doris, that is. Sitting up, she laid the heavy film encyclopedia across her lap and began poring through the entries, but there was no listing for McDougal.

Doris was the only person I met in Hollywood who really deserved fame and fortune, she thought with a frown. It would be just terrible if she didn't make it. Kiki leafed through the book, glancing over the photos. But all she could find were pictures of famous movie stars. There were Clark Gable and Claudette Colbert, Spencer Tracy and Gina Gerome . . . "Wait a minute!" Kiki cried out loud as she stared at the photo of Gina Gerome. Those eyes, that crooked smile—why, it was Doris! Kiki laughed with delight. I guess her Hollywood make-over was just the opposite of the one MGM did on me, she thought. The studio had done away with her bleached hair and heavy makeup and turned her into a beautiful brunette.

Eagerly, Kiki read over Doris's entry in the encyclopedia. "Gina Gerome (formerly Doris McDougal, 1918–1979) was well known for her sassy, sexy, sidekick characters who earned her the name of the Brunette Bombshell," the book said. And there was a quote from Doris at the bottom of the page. "Me, a star?" it said. "Why, heck, I'm just a farm girl from Kansas who likes to ham it up in front of the camera. In fact, I never would have gotten into the pictures at all if it hadn't been for the help of a special friend of mine—someone I never got a chance to thank."

That's me! Kiki realized with pride. She smiled with satisfaction. So Doris *did* become a star after all. And she deserved it, too.

But there was one more person Kiki wanted to look up in the book.

197

Flipping through the K's, she found the entry on Kyle. There was a photo of him kneeling in front of Grauman's Chinese Theatre, his face and chest covered with cement. Kiki couldn't help laughing. Boy, would he be mad if he knew *that* was how the public remembered him half a century later!

To Kiki's surprise, there was only a small entry for Kyle. "Kyle Kirby (1914–1980) was an appealing leading man who made a few good movies and then dropped out of sight," the encyclopedia said. "According to gossip columnist Louella Parsons, his nerves just couldn't handle the hard life of a star. After his last picture, *Stars in Her Eyes*, he became jumpy and high-strung and eventually retired to a small farm in the country, far from the bright lights of Hollywood."

So, Kiki thought with a sly smile, I guess watching me disappear right before his eyes kind of flipped Kyle out. Well, it serves him right!

Closing the book, Kiki lay back on her bed. A few minutes later, the doorbell rang. Kiki glanced at her bedside clock. Good old Steve, always on time, she thought.

Kiki got up and ran downstairs. Steve was in the foyer, talking to Mr. Wykowski. At the sound of Kiki's footsteps on the stairs, he looked up, and as their eyes met, he broke into a loving smile. Oh Steve, Kiki thought, her heart almost bursting with joy, I love you. She jumped down the last two steps and came to stand by his side.

"And what are you two doing this evening?" Mr. Wykowski asked. "Going out?"

"Not tonight," Kiki replied. "There's some old movie on TV that Steve wants to watch." She took Steve's arm. "Come on. Let's go make some popcorn."

Once they were alone in the kitchen, Steve took Kiki in his arms and asked, "How's my leading lady?"

The feel of Steve's arms around her made Kiki's heart pound with excitement. "Fantastic!" she sighed. "How about my leading man?" In reply, Steve gently ran his hand over her cheek, then leaned close and kissed her. Kiki kissed him back, savoring the comforting warmth of his lips. At last, Steve pulled away. "Did you have a good time at the dance last night?" he asked, smiling happily.

"The best," Kiki said, thinking back over the beautiful evening. They had spent every moment together, dancing, talking, or just holding hands. When the last song had ended, they'd joined Ramona and Bob for pizza in Westdale Center. And then later, when Steve had driven her home, there'd been that long, lingering good-night kiss . . .

"Kiki," Steve said, leaning back against the kitchen counter, "there's something I've been wanting to ask you."

Kiki took the popcorn maker from the closet and plugged it in. "What?" she asked curiously.

"Remember back when we weren't seeing each other? Why did you wear a scarf and sunglasses to school every day? Everybody was saying you thought you were the next Marilyn Monroe."

"Oh, that," Kiki replied with a careless laugh. Thinking quickly, she said, "Well, uh . . . Jenna and I were playing, and she knocked over a bucket of paint. It got all over me—my hair, my clothes, even my eyebrows. And when I tried to wash it out, no luck at all. It looked so awful, I was embarrassed to let anyone see it. So, uh, I wore the scarf and sunglasses until Mama figured out how to make me look okay again."

"Really?" Steve looked horrified. "Man, I'm glad I don't have any little sisters!" He laughed. "I'm just glad everything's back to normal now." He leaned close and ran his hand through her hair.

"Yeah," Kiki agreed. "It sure was crazy for a few weeks there."

And how! she added silently. She thought back to the hectic days she'd spent in Hollywood—the long hours of filming, the crazy crush she'd had on Kyle, and then the final wrap party when all her fantasies had crumbled to dust.

"So what's this movie?" she asked as the last kernel of corn exploded in the popping machine. She dumped the popcorn into a bowl and added some melted butter and salt.

"Something called *Stars in Her Eyes*." Steve picked up the bowl and headed toward the living room. "The listing in the paper said it was a vintage thirties tearjerker."

Kiki froze, panic gripping her throat. Somehow, it was hard to believe that the movie actually existed. Was she really about to see herself on TV, starring in a movie made half a century ago?

"I've never heard of it, have you?" Steve continued. He turned around. "You coming?"

Kiki gulped, following behind him. What if Steve recognized her as Aileen Adair? Her heart pounded in her ears. How would she explain what she was doing in a film made in 1939? "Steve, are you sure you want to watch this?" she squeaked.

Steve put the popcorn down on the old wooden coffee table. "Oh, it'll be great. Those cornball love stories they made back then were loads of fun." He drew Kiki close to him. "I think we're probably missing the credits right now." Before Kiki could utter another word of protest, he clicked on the television.

Kiki didn't dare breathe. But as soon as she caught a glimpse of herself in the first scene, she knew she had nothing to worry about. Not only would Steve not be able to recognize her—she could barely recognize herself! Her platinum bleached-blond hair, plucked eyebrows, and heavy makeup completely changed her face. Her thirties-style dress was a far cry from the jeans and O. Henry High sweatshirt she was wearing now.

But the biggest difference was her voice. Thanks to the breathy voice Marty had insisted she put on, she could barely understand what she was saying on screen.

Apparently, Steve couldn't, either. "You know, that Aileen Adair looks a little like you," he said. "But her voice—whew! She sounds like she just got finished running the Boston Marathon."

I *felt* that way sometimes, Kiki thought, reaching for a handful of popcorn. Kiki rested her head on Steve's shoulder. It was so odd to watch herself acting in an old movie. The plot was unbelievably corny, and the overblown music only made things worse. Still, Kiki decided, it wasn't really bad, just kind of old-fashioned. And maybe someday, if I work hard and keep trying, I'll get another chance to act in a Hollywood film. Only this time, she promised herself, I'm going to use a normal voice!

After the last scene had rolled across the screen, Steve turned to Kiki and said, "I know this is going to sound crazy, but the more I watched that Aileen Adair, the more she reminded me of you. It was something about the way she walked and the way she moved her hands. A few times, I almost caught myself thinking she *was* you."

Kiki laughed lightly, as if the thought of her and Aileen Adair having anything in common was unimaginable. "But tell me," she couldn't resist asking, "do you think she's talented?"

"Aileen Adair? Yeah, definitely. In fact, she was the only thing that made that film worth watching. You know, I can't figure out why she never became a big star. I mean, whoever heard of Aileen Adair?" Steve frowned thoughtfully. "I wonder what ever happened to her."

Kiki curled closer to him and entwined her buttery fingers with his. "Yeah," she said with a knowing smile, "I wonder . . ."